Valentino & I

Timeless love

Youcanprint *Self-Publishing*

Titolo | Valentino & I (Timeless love)
Autore | Anna Piccolini

ISBN | 978-88-92673-72-4

Youcanprint Self-Publishing
Via Roma, 73 - 73039 Tricase (LE) - Italy
www.youcanprint.it
info@youcanprint.it
Facebook: facebook.com/youcanprint.it
Twitter: twitter.com/youcanprintit

Acknowledgements

I'd like to extend a brief thank you to everything in my life which has lead me to new and exciting pathways. I apologize for not having dedicated time and pages to acknowledgements and long prefaces, but I'm a pragmatist, and like to get straight to the point via the shortest and most logical route. I will thank those who assisted me by inserting them into the story. They'll recognize themselves.
I love you all.

Translate By Samuel Battye Rizzardi

June 30 … 8:00 am

Something smells different. It's the smell of seawater. How is this possible? I live in the countryside, where the odor is quite distinct. It can be pungent of course, but not like this.
I open my eyes, but I don't recognize this place. What's going on?
Maybe I'm not fully awake yet, but this feels so real.
My God, now I see. I'm at your house. How is that possible? I'm no longer...

May 17 2014

I keep asking myself why I bothered to start this manuscript, but following my instincts has lead me to discover a new dimension. I'm happy now.
It hasn't been easy. Expressing your most heartfelt feelings takes a good dose of courage, but with love as your guide, everything becomes easier.
Your emotions race from your heart to your mind, and try to imprint themselves in a text which can be understood by someone other than yourself, someone who you'd like to share your experiences with.
All of us have felt these emotions, and not just for people, but also for our beloved four-legged friends.

May 21 2014

Here I am, the eldest of two children! Actually, I'm the third, as I lost two sisters before I was born. They bore my name, but that wasn't due to any lack of my parents' imagination; they just wanted their daughter to be named after my grandmother. I know that in writing this, it all seems so unusual and the perfect recipe for a "weird" life, but let me tell you that I love my life precisely because there is nothing usual about it. It may even seem chaotic to the untrained eye, but my way of letting my imagination run wild every minute of my life makes it incomparably wonderful.

I'm still alive! I say this to all the superstitious ones. Up until now, the odds have been squarely in my favor.

Of course, I've been on the brink many times, but if I'm still here there's a reason for it. I've only just realized that it's my birthday in a few days. I feel that something special's afoot this year.

But let's not get sidetracked. I'll tell you about some of the main events of my life. Life is to be lived, and something good's always bound to happen if you let yourself be guided by it.

Let's see. I'll start by telling you of how I had a rather serious accident at age two.

We were going on vacation with our open-air Dyane. The truck in front of us lost some barrels of oil, which tumbled onto the road. The car swerved and we fell into a ditch. My mother told me of how I was catapulted to the ground from the open soft-top. I was found unhurt and with a big suitcase beside me. She always says how I had been protected by an angel. That angel certainly had his work cut out for him!

In any case, he who starts well is only halfway through. For good or ill, what happened to me made me who I am, and I like how I turned out; a free spirit. I have no chains, and nor do I want any.

My life as a daughter has allowed me to understand what people avoid saying and what they would like to hear. It has made me sensitive and empathic.

Exposing yourself (metaphorically of course) is obviously really hard.

Human nature is complicated, made up of many glitches which render us unique and beautiful in the eyes of others. What counts is loving yourself precisely for your uniqueness. It's a pity I can't get to know you, dear reader of this "book". Perhaps it's a little pretentious of me to call this a book. I am of course under no illusion of being an author. I'm simply a person expressing her thoughts and feelings via a Word document.

I'm growing up, and high school's the place where I found my first love, or rather, I fell in love for the first time at age eleven. His name was Mirco, and I believe he now works for a publisher.

He was a really cute kid. I owe him my life, as he stopped me from crossing the road while the traffic light was red. I'm in your debt, Mirco. If you ever need anything, I'll be happy to be of service.

I'm grown up. At nineteen, I moved from a rather central area of Milan to Famagosta Street with my parents. It is here that I have my third "intervention".

I was lost in thought, and made the same mistake I'd made with Mirco, though I have no idea who it was who dragged me back to the footpath. When I looked behind me, still shocked at what had happened, there was no one there. Who had it been?

I need to make an important confession: *I'm a wimp!*

I'm afraid of the dark, of ghosts, of anything I can't perceive. When I hear something, my mind usually provides a logical explanation, but it couldn't come up with one in this case. I still ask myself what happened to this day.

I'm divulging all of this just to show you that I'm not unfamiliar with strange events, but I would never have imagined what I'm about to tell you.

May 22 2014

The days plod on, but at least there are cooking courses every evening. We've been doing this course for seven years now, and my husband is the chef. He's the most skilled person I've ever known. He's a professional not only in his art, but as a teacher too. He's understanding and always has much to impart. He's really one of a kind. He's not a big fan of the media, so he's never wanted to appear on TV or write a cookery book.

Getting back on topic, I've lately been developing a strange interest in Rudolph Valentino.

After watching a TV series on his life, I caught a glimpse of some of his photos. I must say, he wasn't all that attractive under makeup. Later on, I watched some of his short movies, some YouTube clips, and countless images. Wow: he's gorgeous!

I can positively state that Valentino is a melting pot of genetic exceptionality.

My curiosity only deepened as I continued my research.

Everything about him can be accessed online, even clips on his death. The weirdest thing is that some people assert that they can see him still, and that he manifests himself as some kind of Latin lover.

Hallucinations no doubt.

And so, doubtful and confused, I lose myself navigating through 1920s celluloid.

I began this research because I've always found the twenties fascinating, from the car designs to the clothes, particularly the shoes.

Even the leisure activities were marvelous, and especially the flappers; bob-haired girls who loved dancing the Charleston in the open. Pretty much everything was wonderful in the Roaring Twenties!

I found out through my research just how much Rudolph Valentino liked to joke around.

And so, this morning, as I lay in my bed refusing to get up, my tablet made a strange noise.

I honestly couldn't care less for that sound, but something inside me compelled me to investigate.

Upon activating it, I noticed that a Google page I hadn't selected had been opened.

I stared at the screen in confusion before shutting it.

A few seconds later, I heard another chime.

Increasingly perplexed, I reopened the screen and saw that it displayed "Falcon Lair", Rudolph Valentino's house.

Such a shame it's no longer with us!

Just to check it wasn't just some pop-up, I opted to keep the tablet on. Maybe it was just me accidentally pressing something.

It was at that point that panic set in, as the device began streaming images of Valentino's old house without my doing anything.

I asked myself what was causing this, but I honestly couldn't think of anything. My fear was however accompanied by a strange euphoria.

I felt so disturbed I slept in a different room after shutting the tablet down.

Only later, after having digested all that had occurred, did I go and rewatch some Valentino clips. Everything seemed normal again.

June 26 2014

Night had fallen and I was again lying in bed, with images of the videos I'd watched flashing through my mind. I was puzzled, yet fascinated. I couldn't explain why I felt this way. He was undeniably an interesting figure, but long dead! I had no reason to be attracted to him.

I thought about how nice it would have been to know him.

That one idea would clash with one of my greatest fears. A part of me couldn't believe what I was about to do.

I extended my arm and spread my fingers, wishing strongly that he'd clasp them into his own.

Was I really asking to be touched by a ghost, or at least see one?

This really went beyond any concept of strangeness I'd ever had.

June 29 2014

I spoke of these strange events to a student at the cookery course. She's been my friend since childhood, and is the self-styled daughter of a "soothsayer". I've known many people with extraordinary abilities, so perhaps this is another milestone in my life. Nothing happens by chance.

Cecilia (for that is her name) doesn't charge, and offers her services for free. I sense I can trust her.

I have an appointment at her office at eleven on Monday. I don't know what to expect, and I ask myself what the point is. She'll be curious to know what's going on.

I've never been so shaken.

8

July 1 2014

Another day has passed. Last night I downloaded a bunch of songs I enjoy and listened to them with my headphones. Night approached, and those romantic melodies made me picture Valentino's face, his smile, that special simplicity of his, a simplicity that's almost too good to be true.
As my face brightened, I felt the shoulder of the robe I'd just put on slide down. Shocked, I immediately put it up. I couldn't explain why, but it kept falling.
It was embarrassing, as I felt the hem of my robe lift. I got angry, and my heart raced insanely. Someone was obviously with me. It was an odd way of announcing oneself, that's for sure!
I longed for something more to happen, but perhaps it was too early.

July 4 2014

I type furiously on the keyboard as if it were a harpsicord, opening up my heart. I'm alone in the room, listening to music, however...
Something odd's happening. My God! I feel like someone's lightly caressing my arm.
What should I do?
I continue typing, hoping it won't stop. It's difficult to maintain my composure. I just don't get anything anymore. It's a real person stroking me.
Slowly, I feel it creep to my hand. It lifts and I feel fingers clasp between mine.
I feel energized. I want to express myself, but I can't. That would be embarrassing. My heart longs for it to be Rudolph Valentino.
Ten minutes of pure ecstasy passed. But where was the fear? It was a ghost after all! Perhaps its absence was due to the specter being invisible.
I should be terrified, but I'm so happy. It's the most wonderful sensation one can have.
Please, don't go! Stay with me.

Tears well from my eyes, and not just from joy, but from a sense of loss.

Where are you? Why did you leave? Touch me again, I'm not afraid. I want to feel your hand on mine again.

I wish with all my heart that you could break down the "barriers" and return to me. If it won't happen tonight, then I'll see you in my dreams.

Tomorrow you'll be in my every thought.

But wait a minute.

What if it isn't Valentino? What if it's someone I'd find unattractive?

Enough thinking. See you tomorrow.

July 5 2014

As absurd as it may sound, I think I have feelings for him, even though I can't see or touch him. My heart tells me that this mysterious presence is indeed Rudolph Valentino. I continue searching for online images. For me, the perfect ones are those where he looks imperfect, a bit chubby with dark rings around his eyes. I love imperfections.

I'm behaving strangely. I've changed. I have become romantic, to a point totally at odds with my character. I stare into space, but it isn't empty to me, knowing that he's there.

Now his bouts of touching me are becoming more frequent. My face lights up during those moments and I smile without reason.

I would never have thought I could be so happy over such a bizarre situation.

Now that he's here close to me, I don't see him, but I smile anyway. There's no need to see when he's close; one only needs love-struck eyes.

I feel goosebumps on my arm as he touches me. I think he wants to kiss me too.

This is incredible! Who knows when I'll be able to see him?

I obviously thought of the possibility of having a screw loose, and conducted some experiments.

Last night, for example, I went blindfolded to a closed door and asked him to place my hand on the doorknob and lead me into the bathroom unharmed. I never lost hope.

All that's missing is my returning his caresses. I can only imagine him moving my hand in empty air, his motion like a stroke on the cheek.

It's a dream! I can physically tell that something's not right, but it's not my skin. What will physical contact with him be like? Cold?

At least that's what I think. I've seen many TV documentaries on these entities, and they all say that their presence can be detected by drops in temperature.

This is the perfect opportunity to test this, seeing as it's so warm!

I discover that it gets hotter whenever he approaches.

I can't spell out my feelings accurately. I know it's crazy to say so, but he's without a doubt my greatest friend.

July 6 2014

He's really something else. I can't see him, yet he excites me.

At first I thought the voice in my head was just my conscience. It was he who corrected me.

It's he who raises my spirit, telling me that we'll find a way to meet up in this plane of existence.

I can't wait to hug him so tight he'll choke, and drown him in kisses.

That night, I curl up on the edge of the bed, giving him room to lie next to me.

"Will I be able to see your face on my pillow, my love?"

I know you say you don't have the needs of a living person, but I'll never stop hoping to see you by my side when I wake up.

Tonight, when you wake me, I want to kiss you back, my lips to yours, look you in the eyes and tell you what I feel.

Something strange happens. He moves my hands from the keyboard.

Entity: Let's do away with all this doubt. I am Rodolfo Raffaello Guglielmi, otherwise known as Rudolph Valentino.

He writes: It's all very strange to me too, and I'm constantly surprised that you keep looking at me, even without seeing.

You can stop asking where I am now. You know the answer.

I love you more than you can imagine. I have no idea how two totally different destinies could cross paths this way. I know it's absurd, but I wouldn't want to be anywhere else right now.

I thought I'd be at peace, yet I still feel the same things I did as a living person. I love! Love is driving me crazy and I can't stop thinking about you. I'll never leave you. I watch you while you sleep, and sometimes I'm so worked up with passion that I kiss you, but I'm so rough that I end up waking you. I know you're no longer afraid of me, but I realize I might scare you a little if you saw me. We'd spend countless moments just gazing at each other, but that's all I want. My romantic side is exactly like my Latin lover persona. I think making love with all this baggage would be incredible. I love this existence with you.

You know how to use a keyboard!?

Seriously, you said you love me, but you've barely got to know me.

Rudolph: I can't explain it all. Just realize that there is no fixed period of time needed to fall in love with someone. What do you feel?

I don't want to think too much right now. I'm just so happy over what you've written and confused about what's going on with me.

Rudolph: Consider it a game. Nothing's impossible for you. Space, time, it's all one reality. Make everything simpler and don't complicate things obsessing over the difficulties. Everything is possible. You're really special.

Lots of women dream about Rudolph Valentino, and it seems impossible to me that he's here.

As I was walking with a friend of mine (the first to read what I had written), I was hit by something I couldn't explain. As she spoke, I found I couldn't listen, for I felt Rudolph's overpowering presence. It's fantastic!

While leaving work by myself, I felt as if I were flying while listening to the music on my cellphone. I saw things I'd seen before with new eyes. Everything gleamed. The leaves seemed greener, and I felt that the world was sharing in my joy. I want to be alone today and savor these sensations. I still can't figure out why he chose me. Can it really be Rudolph Valentino?

I've always believed that if you want something strongly enough, events will conspire to make that wish a reality, but I never thought that things like what's happening now could come true.

I'm sat in front of the computer, and I miss him terribly. I want to see him. I really want him to come to me.

It's true that, as he said, I'm terrified, but being afraid is better than all this waiting.

I sometimes ask myself if these eccentricities of mine are a part of falling in love. Maybe I should get back down to earth and work out what's causing this mental instability, but I can't. I feel like a young girl again. What a wonderful feeling love is!

I feel like a torrential river. I could never stop talking about him and my feelings.

My friend Debora wants to read the sequel to find out how it ends. Imagine how I feel, waiting impatiently for the moment in which I get to know him. For now I can only wait. As painful as it is, it's somewhat arousing.

I don't know what will happen, but I'm sure it will be beautiful, and that's enough for me.

Evening has come, and the cooking classes are about to start. This time I'll be happier than usual, even while I'm counting the minutes until I can go to bed and dream about him, hug myself

with his memory and fall asleep with a smile on my face, knowing he is near.

July 8 2014

Last night's barbecue course went well. There were lots of nice
people there, and soon the summer vacation will start.
We're all rosy, though I doubt the sun can explain why I look so
flushed.
I liked a recipe which unfortunately got lost in the earlier editions. I thought it would be fun to share it here.
Voilà!

Beer-marinated wieners

4 wieners
½ liter of beer
Salt, pepper and herbs

Brown the wieners with the herbs on the BBQ at medium-high heat. Add salt and pepper.

Get an aluminum container containing beer and warm it on the grill. When the wieners are almost done, pierce them and place them in the warm beer. Let them stew for 20 minutes.

Through osmosis, the beer seeps into the wieners whilst allowing the fat to bleed out.

A summer delicacy, perfect for get togethers.

Tonight's class will be on seafood, though I'm allergic to it.

I have tons to prepare for Gianluca's arrival and departure. Apart from being a famous chef, he's a renowned baker. He's a really nice man, humble and unpretentious. We both love fooling around and have a craving for whipped cream. I consider him a friend with a capital F. He's really special, and I wish him the best in finding someone just as unique. It's always a pleasure seeing him again.

See you tomorrow.

July 10 2014

I'm alone, going through my daily routine.

The school has a store which sells hard-to-get products for those wanting to bake modern sweet or savory delicacies. The products are wrapped in little confections suited to the buyer. It even has a bathroom, which you need to go through a corridor to get to. There's a door in the corridor leading to a cellar which we don't use, as it's always locked. I believe the building was constructed in the 18th century.

Even though I've somewhat overcome my fear, I'm always afraid when I pass in front of that door, and today I need something from the bathroom.

Darn, couldn't we have walled up that cellar!

My imagination runs wild. Who knows what entities lurk there! You see what I mean by my fear?

I'll need to pluck up all my courage to retrieve the object.

I get up and march on. I'm writing in order to delay getting there. Okay, enough messing around. I'll take my tablet with me, and the moment I get what I need, I'll head for the back of the store and start writing again.

There, done! I can be quick when need be.

Now I'll make myself a warm drink. I have a coffee machine at the back, near the fridges. I've certainly earned it.

My head is lowered. I write and occasionally sip my coffee.

I feel uneasy. I turn my head, sensing something behind me.

I'm writing! I can't move. I keep writing without thinking. I see a pair of brown socks in the corner of my eye.

I'll try to describe what's happening without fainting.

My head's exploding, my heart's about to burst.

Still I write.

Long brown socks, smart, shiny shoes. I can't lift my head anymore; I'm too scared. All I see is a jacket and brown vest.

I can also see some hands; spindly, but very beautiful.

I adore his hands!

Maybe that's what I've noticed the most in his photos.

I feel faint. I recognize that ring.

It's him! Rudolph Valentino.

I switch on the tablet's microphone, knowing that the moment I turn back, I'll lose my senses and forget everything.

Testing, testing. I hope you're recording this.

Now I'm officially crazy, talking to a microphone.

I'm about to raise my head.

I can't look. I'm terrified and giddy at the same time. I'll do it, come what may.

It's him! I shout.

Help! You look alive!

Don't come any closer, or you'll scare me to death.

Am I okay? Everything in order?

No, I've lost it.

Rudolph: Weren't you looking for me?

You can talk? Please, help me. I'm shaking all over.

Rudolph: I've been waiting.

Are you out of your mind as well? Waiting for what?

Rudolph: For you to understand.

I stood dumbfounded.

Rudolph: The answers you want are within you. Can I come closer?

Are you crazy? Let me do it! My God, you're even more handsome in life than in the photos.

What have I just said? In life? I guess I can still be comedian even while panicking. Would you believe it! I don't know whether to laugh or cry.

I hope you're still recording

I approach without fear. Everything's normal...

It's better if I pass this off as normal. Please, help me by saying you're from some different dimension or something.

I keep babbling nonsense. It doesn't get crazier than this.

Rudolph: I can't. This is your dimension.

You're a big help!

I keep joking to break the tension.

I think.

No, that's not it. I feel panic rising.

I'm calm, it's just a normal friend who's come by.

Calm down, calm down!

I've taken a step. The next will be shorter.

I'm closer now. Stop!

My heart is racing. I'm not so scared anymore. You really do look alive.

Rudolph: May I touch you?

No, I'll do it. Give me your hand.

It's not cold! Shouldn't it be?

Rudolph: Not in this case. Can I touch your face?

Let's give it a try.

If you keep this up, you'll kill me. This feels so nice. You're good.

Rudolph: Thank you.

Please, don't stop.

Rudolph: I don't intend to. Can I touch your arms too?

Do what you want. Wait, let me lock up the store and put the closed sign on. Don't disappear.

Rudolph: You know I won't.

I'm back!

Rudolph: I want you in my arms.

Go ahead, it's all so fuzzy now. I just can't believe this is real. I'm breathing fast, I can't help myself.

Rudolph: Be quiet!

I'm really embarrassed. His lips are too close to mine.

Rudolph: You're mine. Have you got anything to say?
I'm under shock. This all seems so impossible. He's kissed me.
Tell me, why are you doing this?
Rudolph: What do you think?
I think you feel what you wrote to me.
Rudolph: There you go!
Dammit, they're knocking on the door. I must open it.
Shall I see you again?
Rudolph: What do you think?
I think so.
Rudolph: Wait for me.
You can be sure of that. Kiss my hand again before I go.
Thank you.
Rudolph, wait! I feel something for you too.
Rudolph: I know. I haven't forgotten what you told me.
It would take more than a pinch to convince me that this isn't all
a dream.
You can't imagine. He's unusually handsome.
He's tall, about 1, 76. I think he wears size 8.5 shoes. He's got
magnetic, brown-colored eyes and chestnut hair. There's a small
scar on his right cheek. His face is smooth. The smell of his skin
is enticing, but rather snuffed out by the perfume he wears. He's
so elegant, elegant in a dreamy way.
I didn't know you could smell perfume on a ghost, but then
again even the warm hands were a surprise!
It's the first time I've ever encountered something so out of the
ordinary, and so all my preconceptions are down the drain.
I need to get a grip of myself and keep writing. I feel like I'm on
cloud nine. I'm in tilt!
I can still feel his lips on my hand, his gaze upon me.
The mere thought of him distracts me.
You can't imagine the idyllic sensation I felt when he kissed me.
It was as if those incredibly soft lips enveloped me completely.
He held me tightly to him. A total transcendence. The world dis-
solved around me. I could no longer understand anything. It's as
if I've known him always.
Infinity, space and time had vanished. I didn't want it to stop.

I'm here now, and as I think of him, a tear wells up in my eye, as I don't know when he'll return.

We can't set a date and we can't call each other. I can only hope that you manage to return to me.

I beg you, come back. I miss you terribly.

Everything's returned to normal. The course is ongoing.

I can't help but think of him. I fool around with the students in order to seem normal. It's a good thing I'm not the one in charge of the lessons.

I can barely even put a plate in the dishwasher.

As I said, today's theme is seafood. We have an excellent octopus recipe. I'll write it down to distract myself, but it's hard.

He's here! I've got goosebumps. He's touching my hand! I obviously can't see him, but I assure you I feel him!

How can I connect? I keep still.

Keep going, please.

He's moved my hair and is kissing my neck. I get the shivers. I mustn't lose my head.

Thank you for coming back. It's okay if I can't see you. It's enough that you've returned.

At this rate, I'll soon lose control!

It's just so lovely. His hand's descending.

No, don't! Please, I'll lose control.

I get up, not being able to continue.

Rudolph, read what I'm writing.

Stop, I can't take it. Let's do it when we're alone.

Write if you've understood.

Rudolph writes: Yeah, I get it, but I want to be with you. I want to be close to you. You can't imagine how hard it was to get to you. I could see you, but I couldn't talk to you. I wanted you to feel my touch. The more time flew, the more I fell in love with you. Now that I'm here, I can't help myself.

So you really love me?

Rudolph: What do I need to do to make you understand? Didn't you see how my eyes shone when you looked at me? I'm still asking myself how all this is possible, but it's not so important all things considered.

I love it when you write to me. I've decided to include it in this story.

I'll encrypt the file with a password, that way no one will read it.

Rudolph: What do you mean?

Of course! You're from another era.

Rudolph: Silly.

It means I'll insert a question which only I can answer. It will be activated when I open this document, and you'll be able to continue writing, seeing as you're able.

Rudolph: And not only in that!

Indeed. You're acting wasn't bad, and you danced fairly well.

Rudolph: Thank you, but I had something else in mind. Anyway, I could teach you to tango if you like.

I'd like that! It's always fascinated me, just like all aspects of the 1920s. Tell me what it was like.

Rudolph: We have a lot to discuss. You'll see I'll do much more. In any case, we had writing machines too.

I know.

You can stroke me if you like, but only on the arms and face please.

Rudolph: I promise.

I'm off to pretend to work. Tomorrow morning I'll stay at home on some pretense. Will you be there?

Rudolph: I'll try.

Goodnight.

Rudolph: Goodnight, and dream about me.

Yes sir!

Rudolph: I'll think of you and watch you sleep.

How long till tomorrow? I'm smiling like a child. I'm off, I'll shut the tablet down.

Thank you God for this beautiful gift!

July 11 2014

I'm home. I've done my exercises, had my shower, and now I'm all fragrant.

I won't bother making myself up. He likes me as I am.

The bed's comfy. When will he come?

It's now eleven. I need to get dressed for twelve.

Where are you, Rudolph?

Come on, we can be alone now!

Please, the idea that we can't see each other again frightens me.

Time flies. It's almost midday. I'm like a spinning top; I can't keep still. I get the feeling it's going to be a no show.

I feel like a glutton in front of a sweet stall he can't reach, as it's behind glass.

I really need to go.

Rudolph, wherever you are, find a way to come back to me.

July 12 2014

I'm home. It's been days since I last saw you, and I've lost all hope of seeing you again. I miss you terribly.

I saw on TV that they're using microphones to capture sounds from other dimensions.

I'll give it a try!

Last night we covered preservatives. This is the course I like less, but it's definitely useful. One must be vigilant for botulism.

I've been out and about since this morning, and I'm shattered. I've only stopped to write further.

I'm wearing a tennis miniskirt and a shirt which clearly shows I'm not wearing anything underneath. I'll put on my bra now. I'll be back soon.

I turn on the microphone and murmur my thoughts and more.

You're here? But I can't see you. Rudolph?

Rudolph: Yes, I'm here.

I'm still afraid of ghosts, Rudolph.

Rudolph: I'm not a ghost. I'm Rudolph.

Sorry, I know that. Just don't appear, please.

Rudolph: Alright, but do you hear me?

Yes, where are you? On the ground floor?

Rudolph: Yes.

Why?

Rudolph: I want you to come to me.

I can't, I'm scared.
Rudolph: Get down here, you wimp! Do you remember how I kissed you?
Yes.
Rudolph: What was it like?
Lovely.
Rudolph: Would you like me to do it again?
Yes!
Rudolph: Don't you think it would be easier if you could see me?
Yes!
Rudolph: Well then, don't you need to go downstairs to do so?
Yes!
Rudolph: Will you try?
I'm going down the stairs. I can't see you.
Rudolph: I'm on the couch.
Ah right. It's on the opposite side.
I'm scared.
Rudolph: I'm dressed as I was in The Eagle, *a movie you like.*
That's fantastic, but I'm still afraid.
Rudolph: Don't you have a blindfold or something?
Yes, the eyemask I sleep with when there's too much light.
Rudolph: Get it and put it on when you get down from the stairs.
Let's give it a go.
Okay, now what?
Rudolph: Turn around and walk straight on.
And what will you do? I'm scared.
Rudolph: Shut up and do it!
What if I trip?
Rudolph: Don't fret, I'll guide you.
Where are you? Why won't you talk?
Oops, thank you. I'd have fallen if it wasn't for you.
Oh my God, you're all over me!
Rudolph: I'm afraid so. Raise your head.
I'm panicking. These passionate kisses won't do.
Put me down! This isn't one of your films.
Rudolph: True. At least this is real.
Put me down or I'll slap you.

Rudolph: Take your mask off first. I can assure you that you look like Wladimir in The Eagle.
You're starting to annoy me. Put me down!
Rudolph: What, are you getting angry?
Stop it!
Rudolph: Geez, it took a slap on the face, but at least you've taken the mask off and are now in front of me without fear.
Dammit, you're right!
Let's move on to *The Son of the Sheik*: I hate you!
Rudolph: No, let's stick to The Eagle: *I love you.*
You'll end up like Count Torriani.
Rudolph: Would you like to be without me?
Cheeky. No, now that you ask.
Rudolph: I saw you exercising.
Are you changing subject now? Now that I think about it, can you watch everything I do?
Rudolph: Yes.
Well, that's embarrassing. Everything?
Rudolph: Where are you going?
This is unreal. Even when I'm having a bath?
Rudolph: You think I couldn't? That's the perk of being in this condition!
Stop hitting me. Man, you're rough.
That's only half of it. Take your hands off me!
Rudolph: You didn't have a problem with them before.
The last time was fun because I couldn't see you. It's all too real now.
It's all going too fast.
Rudolph: What if I disappeared entirely?
You're right. I keep forgetting that our dates aren't exactly ordinary.
I'm beginning to wonder if you're trying to manipulate my feelings.
Rudolph: I'll explain everything upstairs.
Okay, but why won't you use the stairs?
Rudolph: I don't feel like it!
Lazybones.

Rudolph: Come on, I'm waiting.
Wait! It's a good thing the bed won't break.
No, don't tickle me, please. Stop it, please. I know you're trying to put me at ease, but I'll get an asthma attack at this rate.
Stop it. No, keep going. I love how you kiss my neck.
Rudolph: Your voice is so husky. I like how your breathing gets louder.
I'll stop at this rate.
Rudolph: I've seen you naked, but touching you is really something else.
Your kisses feel so wonderful. Promise me you'll do it forever.
Rudolph: You can be sure of that.
Your lips are amazing. I feel woozy.
Rudolph: I can see that.
Yes.
Your hands are beautiful.
Could you take your ring off?
Rudolph: Sorry, I didn't mean to scratch you with it.
Never mind. Just keep going.
Rudolph: I like it when you talk all sensual.
Ditto; it's so deep and gravelly, yet sexy. My God, why didn't we meet before!
Rudolph: It doesn't seem to have been possible. I want to love you in a way I never have before.
Do it.
Why are you stopping?
Rudolph: I want to kiss you and overwhelm your senses.
The phone's ringing. Wait here, I need to take this.
Mum: Hi, can we talk?
I'm having a bath, we can talk later. Thanks.
Rudolph: You liar!
Would you prefer it if I told the truth?
Rudolph: Why the bath?
Because I usually spend about an hour in there, so...
Rudolph: We'll have ourselves to ourselves for a whole hour.
I hope so!
Rudolph: Where were we?

Hurry up and kiss me.

Rudolph: Wait, I want to look at you.

Waiting's exciting, but I want you now.

Rudolph: You're fidgeting. I can see you like it.

You never stop talking.

Rudolph: Careful, you're ripping that sheet!

I don't think I've ever been so worked up before. Now I know where the whole "Latin lover" shtick comes from.

No! The doorbell's ringing. Let's pretend to not be here.

Rudolph, stop, I'm getting dizzy.

Mailman: Registered mail!

I don't get it, I always leave the curtains open even when I'm away. How could he have known that...? Dammit! I left the front window open. Wait here, I'll try to send him off.

Rudolph: At least put some panties on, otherwise it'll be a three-some.

Very funny!

Mailman: Registered mail, ma'am.

My husband's away.

Mailman: I'm afraid it's for you, ma'am. You need to sign.

I'm coming.

Rudolph, don't leave, for whatever reason.

Rudolph: I'll give it a try.

Kiss me! I'll be back in a tick.

You're so beautiful in the photos, but you're absolutely marvelous in life (or whatever state you're in now).

Rudolph, I'm back!

No! I don't believe it, you've gone. What shall I do now?

My eyes are red. The mailman thought I had a fever. Every inch of me wants to make love to you. Come back!

Half an hour's gone by. I really need that bath now. I need to get a grip of myself.

If he turns up while I'm in the tub, even better. I've got it! I'll light some candles. I forgot the microphone.

I'll turn it off.

I'd better not listen to it, or the bath will never do.

Wait, what's that on the bed? His ring. Funny that it's still here.
It's like the one I have, so it should fit me.
It's a bit large. Never mind.
Oh, the microphone. Off!
It's evening, and he still hasn't showed up. I'll kill that mailman. Not only do I need to pay a bill, but he interrupted the best moment of my life. Let's hope things turn out better soon. And to think I was afraid of ghosts.
"I love you," I murmur.
Good night, Rudolph.
Rudolph: Night night. I'll dream of you!

July 13 2014

Good morning World! I've just made love to Rudolph Valentino. It was spectacular! You ought to see him. He's stretching now. His muscles are gorgeous; not overdeveloped like those in the magazines, but still exceptional.
I think I'll work more at home from now on.
Rudolph: Need any help writing?
Sure, write what you're thinking.
Rudolph writes: It's been so long since I've experienced these sensations, but I'm thoroughly in love now, and it's out of my control.
I'd do it all day. Would you?
That's a silly question.
Rudolph: What do you need to do?
Answer some e-mails, anything to show that I'm actually work-ing.
Rudolph: I'll just watch you.
No fair! Stand still, or I'll lose my concentration.
Think of what you'll tell me about the twenties.
Rudolph: I'll try. Will you write what I say?
Of course!
Can I get a kiss?
Rudolph: "That's a silly question."
I can start now.

I need to ask a question: Why did you say you'd dream of me?
Rudolph: Dunno. Maybe it just came out.
I can't stop looking at you.
Rudolph: Knock it off. Come here.
...
Rudolph writes: I love you.
Me too.
We look like two teenage lovers.
Rudolph: We are!
You more than I.
Rudolph: Have you forgotten that I'm 67 years older than you?
No, but you look 35.
Rudolph: So do you.
Charming, but I expect no less from you.
Rudolph: And not just as face value.
You're becoming more interesting by the minute.
Rudolph: I'll stop writing now. I'm busy.
No, don't disappear!
Rudolph: Quiet.
I'll never get back to work, and not just because I'm now tired. It's getting more demanding and I don't think I'll ever get used to making love in this way. Never mind "Mister powder puff"! You're a man, through and through. Hold me tight while I write. I'm happy. I want to cry it out to the world. I wish that these moments never cease.
Can I take a photo of you?
Rudolph: In the nude?
Let's say less is more.
Do you even register in a camera?
Rudolph: Try it.
Look Rudolph, you're in it! I can't believe how naive I've been. I thought we'd need some special device to photograph you. You're not exactly alive, after all.
Let's take one together.
Don't pull that face, be serious!
We're so beautiful. Look at our smiles.
Are you going to tell me now?

Rudolph: Yes.

Can I record you? That way I don't forget anything.

Rudolph: After all you've recorded, that's a pretty dumb question.

Okay it's on. Go.

Rudolph: Where should I start? Oh yes. I love animals, my horses and dogs, especially my Doberman Kabar. He's all black with a few white patches here and there. You'd like him.

Why are you talking in the present tense? He's dead.

Rudolph: For me, he's still around; he, my sweet little Kabar, and my house, the Falcon Lair.

Sorry, I didn't mean to upset you.

Rudolph: You haven't, but he's the being I'm most attached to. After you, obviously.

But can't I see him as I do you?

Rudolph: Sure, but it's a bit complicated at the moment.

What's the matter with you? You look ill! Your eyes have gone dark. How's that possible?

Rudolph: It's nothing. I'm probably just remembering.

Let's call it off then.

Rudolph: No, let me finish. You need to know everything. You must experience the twenties with me.

Okay, I'm all ears.

Rudolph: When I go out every morning, I take my Voisin. It's got one hell of a body, and I rely on myself for repairs. I then go off on my way. I live in 2 Bella Drive.

I know, although that address doesn't exist anymore. Can I sit next to you?

Rudolph: Come here. Rest your head on my shoulder and I'll keep talking... I go to a bar which you ought to try out. It makes great Italian coffee. I park the car a little distance away, do up my hair and put on a fake beard to avoid being recognized. I don't eat sweet stuff, as I'm prone to weight gain, and my admirers want me slim.

To me, Los Angeles looks like that street in Milan with all those stores, though the name escapes me. I've seen it with you in any case.

I get it; Buenos Aires street.

Rudolph: Yeah, that's it. If you picture it with cars from my time, the two places are identical.

Yes, for the Mineralava rally.

Rudolph: What a time. No matter how much I travelled, everyone knew me. Did you know I couldn't speak a word of English when I first arrived in the States?

Yeah, but you did well for yourself. America's the land of opportunity, and it will always have a place for you if you've got something to offer.

Rudolph: Indeed, I even asked for citizenship there. Italy's always close to my heart, how couldn't it be? But America's given me so much. It made me happy and set the course for you meeting me. I've noticed you didn't even know who Rudolph Valentino was.

Forgive me. I love your time, but I didn't know who you were, if not by name.

Rudolph: Right. Time's flown by. What a decade! Every evening was a party. You never got bored. I wasn't always having fun though. Being a workaholic, I got myself in shape every morning, physically and mentally. I didn't get drunk; my figure didn't let me, and as I said before, I gain weight too easily. Excuse me, my excitement sometimes gets the better of me and I end up changing subject.

I've noticed.

Rudolph: Your answers are as clipped as a telegraph's.

I just like listening to you.

Rudolph: I need to go now.

Where to?

Rudolph: You're so nosey. My answer is as it always will be: it's not for you to know!

Alright. I just find listening to you so relaxing, and I like being close to you.

Give me a kiss.

Thanks a lot.

Rudolph: Have fun. Think of me.

You can be sure of that!

July 14 2014

What a splendid day! I'm madly in love. I'm happy. I can hear the pastry course in progress on the second floor. We're going to bake traditional cakes.

It's a wonderful Sunday. The students are chirpy, and I've made friends with them. They've started a WhatsApp group, of which I'm now a member. I can't do anything else today; I need to start working again.

I'll be thinking of you every second of the way. Talking about you comes naturally now. I can't do otherwise. They'd understand my interest in you and think me crazy, seeing as you died in 1926.

Will Cecilia be able to see you? It's going to be tough getting up tomorrow to see the seer.

She lives quite a distance away, so I'll need to be out for 7:30. Luckily, today's course isn't in the evening; instead of finishing at midnight, it concludes at six.

I hope you can hear me, Rudolph. I miss you, and I want to spend every second of my life with you. You're a ray of sunlight in my life.

July 16 2014

I didn't notice you.

Were you watching me?

Rudolph: What are you doing with the microphone?

Recording some ideas, you know that.

Rudolph: What's that you're drinking?

Water. It's so hot today. Why are you sitting on the pouf? Isn't it a bit small for you?

Rudolph: It's alright.

Still busy?

Yeah, very.

Rudolph: Come here and hand me the glass.

Rudolph! You've even soaked my bra.

Rudolph: Well, how about that! We'll need to get you dry. Get a towel, but first take your shirt and bra off.

Nice, but not exactly an original excuse. Then what?

Rudolph: You'll sit on me like a stallion and we'll look into each other's eyes.

But I'm busy! Oh well, it can wait.

You've got lovely eyes, though your ears are a bit pointy. Anyway, they're hardly noticeable when your face is in focus. Why are you staring like that? What's on your mind?

Rudolph: To hell with my ears. Kiss me!

I ask for no more.

You're a little overdressed for my liking. Here, let me take off your jacket. The fashion of your time was incredible.

What a time!

You look good in those clothes, but right now I'm more interested in what's underneath.

I see your vest has one, two, three, four, five buttons. Your shirt feels smooth, and its blue color suits you.

Hands off! Can't you see I'm admiring you?

I'll undress myself.

Rudolph: No, let me.

I feel lost.

Cheeky! I can tell what you're feeling.

Don't worry, the pouf can take our weight. Lean against the wall. Horse riding's such a great sport. What's your riding style?

Rudolph: Western.

Your breathing's quickened. Keep talking, I'm loving it.

Anyway, my favorite style is English.

Rudolph: Don't stop, please.

Fantastic! Wow, I've cried out.

Next time, let's focus more on the foreplay, or they'll think a man wrote this.

Rudolph: So you didn't like it?

You'll never know.

No, don't tickle me.

I like getting straight to the point anyway.

Rudolph: Shall I help you in your project?

After you coming here, that would be yet another miracle!

That's very kind, thank you. But I don't know how that would be possible.
Let's cuddle a little more, then I'll get back to work.
Look how handsome you are.
I've never said as much to a man, but I have no inhibitions with you.
Please, put your shirt back on. It pains me to say this, but I can't spend all afternoon making love to you.
You can't imagine how much I'd like to.
Rudolph: You're a real chatterbox. I like how we can see each other often. When's your vacation?
You managed to come to me, so I'll find a way to spend more time with you.
I love you so much.
Rudolph: And I you.

July 20 2014

Although I'm shattered, I'm going to put the exercise bike to good use this morning.
When I woke up, he told me to put on some headphones. He selected "My immortal" by Evanescence, one of my favorites. Rudolph's learned to use gadgets far in advance of those that existed in his time. I spent the whole day at the cookery school. Gianluca's course was exciting as usual. All the students naturally came at around the same time to register. I managed to chat with some of them, becoming instant friends. Of note are Stefania and the awesome Marisa, who has a real admiration for Gianluca.
Marisa's a ray of sunshine.
With the chatting, shopping and recording done, the course began.
I knew he was with me, but luckily he didn't touch me.
While I was clearing up, I wrote a little note to him saying I loved him. I tore it up.
Upon finishing, I locked myself in the bathroom.
I leaned against the wall and unconsciously tilted my leg.

I gasped when I felt his hands on me, pulling the other leg forward. For a moment, I felt myself lying on my back. My left arm was pulled sideways. When my right was placed upwards, I realized it was a dancing stance. He was invisible, but I could sense it was him. I turned the microphone on to describe what was happening, then my gaze met his. His penetrating brown eyes were staring into mine with that magnetic glare of his. Despite our intimacy, I can't think straight when he looks at me like that. I'm like a love-struck teenager.

If only I could dance with him in some bar in the twenties! I wouldn't care about their opinions over my lack of dancing skills. It would be one of the most fascinating things I could do with him. I'm awash with emotion in his arms. It's incredible how love makes you irrational. A sudden noise interrupted our precious moment, and I left the bathroom.

This situation involves all the senses, a rollercoaster ride of emotions. It's like the patterns on a stock market trend; elevated peaks contrasted by sudden collapses. As I brewed some coffee in the back room, I started crying uncontrollably.

Tears streamed down my face, washing away the makeup I'd used to add color to my cheeks. I relived the short moment I'd spent with him, and my smile reappeared, and with it my good mood.

I never realized he was so romantic. "You're fantastic, Rudolph!" His title of Latin lover should have been clue enough. Being an actor though, it could have simply been his portrayal of some character from one of his movies.

July 21 2014

I can't dedicate much time to him, and I am at a loss for loving things I could tell him.

When we can't see each other, he expresses his affection by touching my face with gentle movements which I can only describe as caresses. Sometimes, when my hand reaches out into space, I feel it vibrate with what could almost be kisses. Of course, this is just a guess, as I can't see him.

It's almost time to go, and I'll miss these moments. I hope I'll be able to forge new memories with this vacation in Tenerife. I'm an optimist at heart, and know that there's always something nice round the corner.

I recall how Alessandra and I laughingly asked ourselves if we'd prefer a slice of Gianluca's cake or make love to Rudolph Valentino.

She opted for the cake. Guess which one I chose?

I excused my choice by saying: "If I'm going to sin, let it at least be with the best!"

It's true therefore that if your subconscious desires something, it will come true. At the time, I thought it was only a joke, with no thought of it becoming a reality. I think the thwarting of our wishes comes about through mental blocks which get in the way of your desires being realized. It's thus obvious why you don't get something if you don't believe in it one hundred percent. When I made my wish, I was calm, happy, without worries. It's simple enough to know which ones are granted; the ones born from childish musings, full of such spontaneity and innocence that it's impossible for the world to refuse them.

I asked the world, and I got Rudolph.

Tonight will be this semester's last course.

It's great seeing those whom I consider friends bursting with joy. Sometimes though, I feel low with them, wishing for Rudolph to be there by my side.

I need to touch him, stroke his skin, and breathe in his breath.

Feeling myself touched merely strengthens my desire for him.

I miss my reality, where physical contact is a form of communication and my emotions can be expressed.

I want more.

I know that he somewhat feels the same way. I sometimes sense his sadness, and this troubles me.

I am anyway thankful for every moment granted to us. It's a miracle. It shouldn't exist, but it does! Only a feeling as strong as love can break down a barrier like distance. I don't know the substance of this distance, but I'm familiar with its name: death.

July 23 2014

I love you to death. I can no longer live without you. Are you reading this? I wrote this on the computer to express how I feel to him, hoping for an answer. All I got was a light touch.
Love has no boundaries or walls. Time is but the graceful beating of wings.
I'm so happy that I posted this on Facebook today:
"Thoughts and words are in complete symphony with the soul when one is happy."
When words pour from the heart, they surround the souls of those around you.
I must talk about him. Maybe he's close by, so I'll start writing.
Rudolph, would you like to spend all night with me?
Rudolph writes: What a silly question.
I knew you'd take the bait.
Would it trouble you if all of this just ended?
Rudolph: I'd die a second time.
What more can I say before such eloquence?
Rudolph: Stay with me.
Can I ask some personal questions?
Rudolph: Sure.
What's your favorite color?
Rudolph: Red.
Which city impressed you most?
Rudolph: Paris.
Why?
Rudolph: I love the Seine, its sounds, the feeling of peace I get watching it. When you gaze upon it, all the background noise just disappears. I love everything about Paris. Lying by the bank of the Seine by evening really captivates your mind and soul in a carousel of emotion. Words can't express just how peaceful it is. What wonderful memories!
Why did you leave then?

Rudolph: Difficult times.
What more do you remember?
Rudolph: The scent of bread in the morning. Nothing compares to waking up briskly and hearing the crunch of a fresh baguette before you're even fully awake. I miss that feeling. I'd forgotten all about it.
I know that you like Paris too. Why?
The Seine stole my heart too, and you described it perfectly. The baguette's also a good reason. Let's say that I'll eat one the next time I visit that river.
It's a shame you can't do the same. Actually, neither could I, as I'm allergic to yeast. It's late, I must go!
See you tomorrow my love, when you kick me out of bed to go on the exercise bike. I never guessed I'd become so sporty, being a slob and all.
You're just what I needed.
Goodnight!

July 25 2014

We've left, and we're stuck in the plane which will take us to Tenerife from Madrid.
It's a mess, we've been waiting for two hours to leave. First they had to replace a wheel on the plane, then someone in the line unfortunately died. The paramedics came, set up a screen, and then carried the body off. Now we're waiting for fifteen late arrivals, who don't even have the decency to be on time after what's happened. The crew doesn't seem to realize that the sixteenth absentee is the dead one. Who knows when we'll arrive? I miss Rudolph!

July 26 2014

It's my first morning in Tenerife, specifically San Domingo, located in the cloudy northern, less touristy region.

We chose the north again because I feel it's better for my parents, who've joined this time. Sun salutation: it's out in force today!

Tai chi is a very lively sport. Since my breathing's improved, I've even been able to run on the spot. I must say that everything's going swimmingly these days. I do however still carry my Ventolin, a medication which I'd previously used for my asthma, everywhere. Luckily, neither does Rudolph. I couldn't live without either of them.

It'll be difficult to see him, but I have no doubt we'll manage.

We're off to Mount Teide today!

Teide's an inactive volcano, and Spain's highest mountain.

The national park surrounding it varies from thick scrubland to quiet pathways. The countless, differently shaped lava rocks look like a stormy sea. In the middle of the path is the real heart of the park: Las Cañadas.

Every year I capture its various shades through the photos I take. The greatest eruption took place in 1798, leaving behind a unique landscape. The last one occurred in 1909.

I hope it doesn't happen again, as I'd like to come and live here on this magnificent island.

For the island's old residents, the "Guanches", Teide was the home of "Guayota", the Devil.

I stop occasionally on the lava-strewn road to meditate.

This time, he'll be with me.

Just knowing he can perceive my thoughts makes me even happier. I've always been comfortable with myself, but I must admit that his presence is delightful, even if it can be embarrassing at times.

I perch on a wall and listen to "My Immortal", our song.

Where were you? Why are you touching my hand?

Rudolph: I wanted to be close to you.

I can barely hear you.

Rudolph: That's because I don't want them to hear me.

I really needed you by my side.

Rudolph: I love you.

The sensations I feel are incredible, even if I can't see him.

If I were a man, they'd all think I had prostate problems, as I'm always in the bathroom. It's actually the only way we can see each other.
We've worked out a way of communicating without being seen: I write all my thoughts on my body with my finger.
For example: I love you. Kiss me. I then see his transparent hand answer on me. He's started writing in English too.
I want to make love to him, but I don't know how. This vacation's certainly a cut above the rest.

We're having fun watching the shows at Loro Parque.
When I get home, I must upload all the albums I created on my tablet to Facebook.
Loro Parque's an immense complex with a plethora of different animals. The name comes from the Spanish word for parrot.
My parents got front row seats to watch the killer whales. Having seen the wet floor, I asked the staff for a waterproof cloak. I was sure that the whales' movements were causing the water to overflow. The cloak turned out to be useless, though luckily I managed to avoid a soaking, which hit my parents and husband instead.
How lucky that it's always hot here.
The sea lions are spectacular. They can do plenty of acrobatic stunts, though the thing I found most entertaining was their clumsy imitation of seals.
This park donates millions of dollars every year to save endangered species. It's worth a visit.
I've been walking all day and taken countless photos. I'm now exhausted, but it's time to go home.

Rudolph is really angry. He claims I ignore him. Indeed, I haven't been thinking of him. He's right, in a way; I could have asked him to squeeze my hand, what with no one else being able to see him.

It wasn't easy to get him to forgive me, but honestly, nothing's simple here.

He's as pessimistic as the literature attests, as he's now worried that I might get tired of him. But how could that be possible? Doesn't he ever look at himself in the mirror? I see him, and he's a miracle of nature. How could anyone tire of gazing at him?

Forever Rudolph.

I'm off for a walk in the country and think happily of him. Till tomorrow.

July 30 2014

What a great invention the shower is. We've found a way to be together. The water rolls off my back, and his fingers touching my lips makes the whole thing even more electrifying.

I didn't know one could love like this, so intensely. The pleasure of your choice is priceless!

This is why life is to be lived. When the weight of the world gets you down, there comes Rudolph!

Off we go to Puerta de la Cruz!

See you tomorrow.

July 31 2014

We've visited corner shops, supermarkets and the Martianez pools. I love vacations. All your problems vanish and your worries cease to be. The only difficulty is writing with the tablet at dawn. Other than that, it's fantastic.

Oh, and before I forget, there can never be enough sex with Rudolph.

I guess you're all asking how he is in that department. I'll sum up with one word: tireless! Thank God for that!

Let's just say that, in our day and age, he'd do well in hardcore flicks. That's the gist of it. What's more shocking is how easily he transitions from being romantic to engaging in "impetuous" sex as he calls it.

To get an idea of Rudolph's physical features, just go on YouTube and type "All I wanna do is touch you Rudolph Valentino", pausing at the moment he gets out of the car wearing only a swimsuit. You'll understand at that point how enjoyable it is making love to him. Like a fairytale! Now I want him with me. You can imagine what my feelings are after writing this.

Oops... Hi Rudolph.

I'd better be off. I need to powder my nose.

I forgot about Santa Cruz today.

Hugs and kisses.

August 1 2014

I'm red all over. I went sunbathing after lunch without any sun cream.

I just wanted a little tan, but things got out of hand and I lay there for an hour.

While I was relaxing, he did something incredible.

I don't know how he did it, since I was in my swimsuit! He literally drove me crazy. To avoid having my cries of pleasure heard, I rushed to the bathroom. I've never felt anything like this before.

He says he loves me too much and that he'd never hurt me.

Read this, Rudolph.

Nothing happened, it was my fault. I should have put the cream on.

On the topic of my safety, he says I should listen to my husband, as I risk "blowing it."

Consider it done!

Till later. To know other certainly exciting physical details, read on. You won't regret it.

I'm at the table and have just eaten some chocos, some cuttle-fish with green mojo sauce and papas arrugadas. They're all delicious, but it's the place that makes it all the more pleasant. We've started our descent from Teide, which we've been visiting again. We found a lovely restaurant among the cluster pines. A real gem. The sun kisses my face, but it makes writing harder. I asked myself what it would be like, so I took my tablet and here I am!

I felt the usual stream of emotions on Teide, and I thank God for all this. Religion doesn't matter. All that's important is being grateful for these wonderful gifts He places before us.

But where is he? He's here! He always is.

After a few precipices and tortuous paths, I got a delicious ice cream from an Italian-run shop at Los Cristianos. I feel greedy today.

Souvenirs? A new rucksack.

To my mum's query over its being second-hand, I answered that I liked its faded grey color and pockets.

Now I'm sat watching the sea at the "Cafeteria Los Roque". This place is nothing special, but I feel attached to it. It never fails to make me feel at peace.

I'd love to have a house here where I could write from the balcony of one of these little huts by the sea.

How cute! A small neighbor's dog is barking at something and distracts me. He's barely bigger than a flea, as I like to say, but he's still audible.

A little white flea. Seen from here, the waves move in such a way that it seems as if someone's combing them. The white foam captures the sea's movements and moves imagination to a world where wishes come true. How could anyone see all this and not be enchanted?

Los Roques will always be in my heart regardless of distance, and perhaps a part of me will stay here.

August 9 2014

We went shopping at Puerto della Cruz again. The differences in price are notable. Everything's cheaper here, even though most of the goods must have been imported. That evening we had dinner at an Italian restaurant with a nice menu. The day would have ended peacefully had there not been moments in the car where my emotions almost got the better of me. Maybe we ought to find ways of staying together more often, as it's hard not to cry out when he teases me. My eyes are always gleaming, and I often smile at what others would say is nothing.

August 10 2014

Today's my parents' anniversary.
We started by going to the beach. I swam among some coves formed by sea-cooled lava. Some are a kilometer beneath the sea. The experience was out of this world, spectacular in every way.
You can see the lava all around you while swimming. The sea has sculpted it to the point of it looking vaguely like rock.
The ocean is freezing, but the marvelous distractions help you survive the initial contact with the water.
I worried that my asthma would have prevented me from swimming, just as it did in previous years in which I jumped into the water, but I made a promise to Rudolph, and so I dove right in. It was beautiful, without any problems. All that sport Rudolph insisted I do has paid off.
I won't forget a second of this vacation; even if I've been unable to see his face, I know he's been beside me.
Now that I see you before me, in that sailor hat and grinning widely because you know what I'm writing, I say:

I'm happy, my love!

I know it's hard to understand, but it's perfectly possible to be crazily in love like this.

Aren't you going to write something too?

Rudolph writes: You're the love of my life. You're mine forever, and this is something no one can change. I can't wait to be alone with you. You were right. It's been lovely gazing at the sea, the lights at night, and holding you. But what do things taste like to one who can't feel anything?

I want to squeeze you, kiss you, and caress your face while the moon shines upon my hand. I wish you could stay forever alone with me.

I'll help you with your book until you can get sorted financially and live alone on this beautiful island you, and now I, love so much.

Don't ever leave me my love, and not simply because I had to do the impossible to be with you, but because you're the only hope our love has to survive death.

I thank all the women reading this book, the women who loved me and will love me in future. You're all marvels of creation. Without you, men like me wouldn't be able to live. You're the reason we exist. Out there is your flesh-and-blood love awaiting you. He may be unattractive, even clumsy, but he'll be your soul mate, just as I am hers.

Her, the woman who fell in love with me without seeing me, not knowing what I looked like.

I could have been as I am in the photos where I'm all made up to look dashing, or I could have had bags under my eyes, with little beauty to show. She could have seen me like in the images where my shyness doesn't show, that same timidity that tormented me as a child due to my big pointy ears. She fell in love without even knowing my true character. She quashed my fears because she didn't know who I was when she fell in love. She only appreciated my personality, the part of me she could detect. How could I not love her!

She's surpassed all my imagination. She loves me, not just my Latin lover persona. She plays rough with me. She succumbs and distances herself when I'm in the mood. She overwhelms me. She's as sweet, sensual and strong as I am. We're similar, and these games drive me crazy. Everything I've done to be with her

has been worth it. I love you. I want you every second. I want every inch of you. Hold me tight, I can't live without you. I am yours, and I wish you'd say the same.
I beg your pardon, I let myself go a bit. At the risk of repeating myself, you must know exactly how I feel. Keep writing.
You've left me speechless yet again. I can't think straight anymore.
I can only tell you quite simply that I love you.
Happy anniversary, mum and dad.

August 11 2014

After a day of visiting the island, we returned that evening to Puerto de la Cruz. All the bars were teaming with people listening to all kinds of music.
A boy singing Elvis Presley songs caught our attention. The impersonation was spot on, and he was no less handsome. He was gorgeous. Some middle-aged ladies on the front row tried to catch his eye. I confess it didn't leave me indifferent. As I listened to his crooning, I felt I was having an out-of-body experience. I turned around, but saw no one.
Sorry Rudolph, I didn't know ghosts could feel jealousy.
Rudolph: I don't know any others, but I do.
Would you like me to tell you what you were thinking?
You're the one who taught me how to look and think in that manner. I'd never looked at men that intensely before you came along. What's the problem?
Rudolph: I get that, but you understand now. There's no need to keep at it!
This feels like an argument. I find it inappropriate, considering we can't see each other.
Rudolph: Sorry, it's been a while. I lost my temper.
Forgive me, it won't happen again. How silly. Here we are, rationalizing the impossible.
Rudolph: Go, you need to eat something. Enjoy your meal.
Thanks. See you later.

August 12 2014

We're off, and as usual I'm crying over leaving Tenerife.
I love this island, and I'll miss it so much. Everything went smoothly on the return journey from Madrid. I'm now on the flight to Malpensa. The only thing making me happy is knowing he's close by.
Hi Rudolph. See you at home.

August 13 2014

We arrived safely, and this time the thieves didn't drop in, maybe because they finally worked out that there's nothing left to steal.
They came twice before, and the most incredible thing is that the *carabinieri* thought that the mess they left behind was actually my fault. And to think I expected them to take fingerprints! CSI, yeah right.
Madness! At every departure, I leave a friend's number, this time Alessandra's, on the table, and inform the thieves that there's nothing worth taking.
The journey ended well, but I miss Tenerife very much.
Waking up made everything better.
I felt happy because he was there, and not just in my heart. I met his smile with my own: good morning my love!
I can't wait to be alone with him, even if it will be just for cuddles.
Another aspect which makes this awakening special is that I slept in in his arms.
I feel him squeeze me and I'm comforted. He leaves me with a warm feeling as I sleep. Now Alessandra will bring back my ferret Shira, after lovingly taking care of her.
My baby is nine years old, which for a human is equivalent to ninety. She's as lively as ever though, like all ferrets. She'll have had the time of her life playing with my friend's children. I just hope she didn't bite anyone.

Now I'm off for a coffee with Alessandra while the others go for an ice cream.
On with the diet!
Till later.

August 16 2014

Rudolph writes: I can never stop looking at you. Love is shining in your eyes. Your smile makes me feel more alive than I've ever felt. I no longer need to breathe or have my heart beat. All that matters is looking at you, and I'm alive, alive and happy in a way I've never been before. This had to happen regardless of whatever pain I had to go through, even death. I'd go through it again one hundred, no, one thousand times. I love you, you're my life, my eternity. I want you, and you're mine.
Love me forever.
It took you a while to figure out that I wasn't drawing an eight on your hand, but the symbol of eternity. That's what I want for us.
I want you every second of your life, and I'll never stop saying so.
I know it sometimes looks as if I'm in a constant state of passion, but I only feel it when I kiss you. When that's not possible, I picture myself doing it.
Don't ever leave me, my love.
What a wonderful feeling it is to be loved unconditionally. How couldn't it be wonderful now that you're here! Thank you for the feelings you give me.
Soon I'll be going to a museum where I'll be able to see your car, and I'll experience a new joy in admiring the 8A model Isotta Fraschini.
I can't take it anymore. I'm so happy I'd smother you with kisses. I'm about to see objects from the twenties, and I'd like you to see them with me.
Will you be there?
Rudolph: It can be done!
Will you?
Rudolph: I meant the twenties.

Excuse me?
Rudolph: I'll find a way for you to experience them.
I don't understand, but I trust you.
Rudolph: I know. I must have done something right. After all, I can see that you've let yourself go and have complete faith in me.
Something? You've enriched my life. What more could I ask for?

August 19 2014

Hi Rudolph. I've been asking myself what you'd have thought of the love songs I listened to this summer.
Rudolph writes: I like them. They bring out the romantic in me. I'd like to thank you for the dance you dedicated to me to the tune of "Stay with me".
Sam Smith's voice reminded me of the times I spent with you. Everything we do is unique.
We've got so much in common. You like dogs, horses and Spain as much as I do. The most surprising thing is your obsession with the Isotta Fraschini. If we'd met in my time, you'd have had the time of your life!
No, I wouldn't have liked to see you die.
Rudolph: I would have healed myself in time rather than letting myself go. I felt trapped in an oppressive lie which stopped me from meeting normal women, only admirers wanting their slice of success.
And if we could?
Could what?
Rudolph: Go back to my time?
Don't talk nonsense. I'd die instantly of asthma and there'd be no thyroid medication.
Rudolph: The way things are going now, you probably won't need it. Haven't you noticed how you don't use cortisone anymore? Your asthma attacks have pretty much stopped. The exercises I insist you do every morning are having their effect.
You breathe easier now, not to mention your diet has improved.
I know it's hard. I've turned your world upside down, but only

because I knew what the result would be. You'll see. You'll feel younger and live with me in the twenties.

You joke too much. If that were possible, we'd change history.

Rudolph: Just a little.

What about your admirers?

Rudolph: Everything will remain unchanged.

Please stop fantasizing. I do enough of that myself.

Rudolph: Dreaming's one of the most enjoyable activities, even in death.

August 21 2014

It's amazing how everything's exceeded my expectations.

I'm sat on the bed after having the most "impetuous" (as he'd say) sex I've ever had, with a dead man no less.

I'm writing because, although I'm fitter than I used to be, I wouldn't be able to do it again.

Repeating this would take the breath away from even a non-asthmatic.

However, my strength comes back just by looking at his captivating stare.

Maybe it would be better to not look at him. He's just too arousing. My mind brims with images of what's just happened, and I can't help but want to repeat them.

A perk of doing it with a ghost is that he never gets tired! Inexhaustible.

It may seem strange of me to say this now, but I love his hands and how they move over my body. They drive me crazy.

I want you to know that he's not hairless like in the photos. I love nice hairy chests.

I don't like men with abs, whatever their age. Of course, a bit of muscle is fine, but only to harmonize a man's body.

Rudolph writes: How lucky then that the only abs I've ever seen have been on beaches!

Cheeky. You know I'm not going to delete what you write.

Rudolph: Who's going to believe you, anyway?

Fine, what's the point in writing this then?

Rudolph: Just to leave a little doubt. Oh, and just to get it off of my chest, I am a heterosexual. You can vouch for that, right?
If only they were more like you.
Rudolph: What do you mean?
I'm just saying. More men should be like you.
Rudolph: And more women like you.
You're being cheeky again!
Rudolph: I'm not kidding!
I don't like transcribing your compliments. I find them a little insincere. At least tell me them in private.
It's not fair! You make me lose track of time this way.
Rudolph: Here's an idea. Seeing as it'll soon be half twelve, I suggest we take some time to get in shape together. What do you say?
You always talk as if you were still alive.
Rudolph: Let me show you just how alive I can be.
I won't bother putting the microphone on then. There won't be much to transcribe anyway.
Rudolph: Excuse us, but we're busy. So long.

August 23 2014

I'm all alone today. He's gone to Los Angeles.
He wants to see the women mourning his death. Even years after dying, it has the power to move him.
He told me of how he wishes to thank them, but there's no way to do so.
What are you doing here?
Rudolph writes: Let me write something for my admirers.
Go ahead.
Rudolph: I adore you all, and I don't know how to thank you all for the love you still show me. You're beautiful and unique. I hope you'll continue to visit me, and if you're no longer in the flower of youth, let me remind you that I had my 199th birthday on March 6, so I'm eager to see you in the years to come.
I thank the woman in red who brought me that beautiful flower.
Thank you all. You're always in my heart, and I love you!

Jealous?
Why should I be? You're a star, and so it's only natural that this occurs.
I just insist on not taking it to the next step.
Rudolph: Next step?
Do you want me to spell it out?
Rudolph: No, I need to go now.
Why won't you kiss me?
I'm thinking.
Rudolph: What's troubling you?
Today in general, and what you must have been going through before dying.
Rudolph: That's all past. Think of the present and wait for me.
Alright.
Till later.

August 26 2014

I'll never get used to being woken up in the middle of the night by someone kissing me so eagerly.
I hope we're not found out.
My friends don't believe in ghosts anyway, so it's not like I'm committing a crime or anything.
I wouldn't call it cheating, and I don't really care either way.
Rudolph: I should think so too!
Hi. Where were you?
Rudolph: Here! I was reading what you wrote. It looked like you were venting something.
I was.
Rudolph: I really like the term 'scruffy'.
I'll have to explain it.
Rudolph: Allow me!
It means that her curly hair doesn't quite know where to go in the morning and juts out everywhere. I find it beautiful, but she calls it scruffy.
Melodramatic as usual.
Rudolph: What do you want to do today?

I'd like to take a stroll, hand in hand.
Rudolph: What if I'm recognized?
No offence Rudolph, but you've been dead for quite a while, and I doubt someone would even know who you are. We could say you're an impersonator.
Rudolph: I'd have liked one before. I had no privacy back then.
Aren't I enough for you?
Rudolph: Yes, sorry, I misspoke. After three months of knowing each other, I think you could let it pass, no?
Of course!
Rudolph: Will we be alone tomorrow?
No, not for a few days.
Rudolph: I miss touching you.
I feel the same.
Rudolph: I'll caress you gently, so that no one notices. I just want you to know that I'm always with you.
I love you.
Rudolph: And I you. Never forget that.

September 1 2014

I'm finally alone.
Where are you?
Rudolph, I can't sense you!
I'm obviously not your priority today.
Oh well, I guess I'll go out, explore the world and meet up with some women... and men.
Oh look, there's someone here.
That got you running.
Rudolph: Obviously. I'm always listening. I'm a Taurus, remember? I'm very possessive, and don't want anyone approaching you.
Alright. Keep telling me about your time.
Rudolph: I see you like the Black Bottom dance of 1919.
That's true. It has some interesting steps.
Rudolph: I think that your real interest is in the Charleston though.

Yes, I love it. You've already seen that I know a few moves, but I'd like to learn it properly. Can you teach me?
Rudolph: I'll think about it.
Cheeky as always! In that case, I'll go to a dance school.
Rudolph: Go ahead!
You're weird. I can never tell what your next move is going to be.
Were you like this when you were alive?
Rudolph: Don't remind me. I wasn't myself back then. I was careless in my choice of women, and I can tell you that Natasha wasn't very loving. It was my fault, really. You must take control of your own life and not be influenced by others. Still, she did some good too. Although she was a perfectionist, she taught me discipline and determination.
Do you know what I really miss? My books!
If I hit the jackpot one day, I'll try and find them.
Rudolph: Thanks. I so want to have them back.
Who knows what became of them! Whoever has them now probably doesn't know how lucky he is.
Rudolph: Maybe he's reading these lines now and recognizes the style.
Maybe. They'll undoubtedly be in America.
Do you know German too?
Rudolph: Not a word!
One website says you had books in German.
Rudolph: True, but I had the English or Italian translations for them, that way they'd help out whilst I read them. In any case, books in their original language have their own flavor.
On the topic of flavor, I've seen that you don't know how to cook. You made a real hodgepodge out of that spaghetti dish!
Rudolph: Let's just say my talents lie elsewhere.
You're right there!
Did you mess around in the kitchen while you were alive as well?
Rudolph: Not much. Not to blow my own trumpet, but I had a chef. Before I was a star, it was sometimes difficult to get any-

thing to eat. I had to tighten my belt too, you know. Anyway, my cherubic face helped.

Cherubic?

Rudolph: I'm hardly an Adonis.

Leave that judgement to the ladies. I think I speak for many when I say you were exceptionally handsome. I prefer you without makeup, as you know. Still, there are some images of you all made up which do you justice.

How did the actresses react to you?

Rudolph: Acting is a profession. You take on a role and you're so absorbed in it that you don't think about the nice-looking man before you. It was the same with me when I had a beautiful woman in front of me.

There are some photos of you with your hands in what you would probably call "impetuous" positions.

Rudolph: It's what the script demanded.

That's all?

Rudolph: Let's not beat about the bush here. Am I a Latin Lover or not?

If I must excuse myself, my brother always said that I was always faithful to the women I loved.

Je t'aime.

Moi aussi.

Do you like today's actors?

Rudolph: Sure, they're good. It's impressive how they totally enter the roles they're given. They manage to act in front of cartoons without even seeing them. Brilliant. Very professional. I like them.

Were things simpler back in the twenties?

Rudolph: Yes and no. You had to know all kinds of gestures linked to emotions. There was no other way to act, but once mastered, it was easy.

Did you like my performances?

Yes, in almost all your films. My favorite is *The Eagle*.

Rudolph: I know that.

It's romantic, adventurous, and has a happy ending.

Thank God for the internet. I wouldn't have been able to find your films otherwise. I'm going to the Verona museum tomorrow. As I told you, it has many relics from the twenties. I'll meet my second love: the 8A Isotta Fraschini.
Rudolph: What's your first love then?
Okay, let me think...
Rudolph: We're like a bunch of kids.
There's no time in moments like these, or age. You're one to talk: you shouldn't even be here!
Rudolph: Why do you think I came?
Because you love me. I think there may be another reason, though. I haven't fully understood it yet, and you're not very forthcoming whenever I ask you about it.
Rudolph: Everything in good time.
There, you see!
When I'm at the museum, will you tell me the history behind everything I see?
Rudolph: With pleasure!
I'll take the microphone with me, of course.
Rudolph: You two are inseparable.
See you tomorrow.
Rudolph: Till later.

September 2 2014

Here we are. I'm waiting for Alessandra. Soon we'll be in the province of Verona.
I'm so happy.
Hi. Are you looking into my eyes?
Rudolph: They're shining!
Yes. I'm on cloud nine.
Rudolph: Let me be your Cicero.
I can't wait!
Rudolph: I'm happy too. I miss so many things.
I'll have my dad give me all his stuff from the twenties. What do you say?
Rudolph: That would please me a lot.

There she is! See you later.
Oops, I almost forgot the microphone. Hugs and kisses!
Hands off! Everyone can see my reactions.
Here we are, at the museum.
The path is long, and my emotions everywhere. Soon we'll buy the tickets. I feel like a little girl again. I'm overjoyed. I don't dare think of what I'll see.
I can use the microphone, seeing as I told Alessandra I need to make a record of what I see and what emotional responses I have. A half-truth.
Microphone on!
There are some cars from the fifties. Wow, a Topolino!
Look Alessandra. These cars are from the thirties.
Oh lord, there it is!
I approach cautiously. I can barely stand. I feel so moved. I'm crying!
It's the most beautiful car I've ever seen.
There it is in front of me, in all its shiny majesty.
It's an 8A Isotta Fraschini, a model from 1929.
How I've waited for this moment. I'll never forget this.
I love this car. What I'd give to see it on the inside.
Getting in is my unreachable dream. Who knows if destiny will ever permit me to sit on that fantastic upholstery?
I'm obviously going to photograph it from every angle. It will be the background of all my social media profiles.
I love you, Isotta!
I shouldn't touch it, so I'll just stroke the hood. I must. I'd never forgive myself if I missed this opportunity.
There are some mechanics nearby. I'll try giving them a sad look. That might convince them to let me go inside.
Excuse me, I'm writing a book set in the twenties, and I'd like to see the inside of the Isotta Fraschini. I won't go in, obviously!
I've come a long way from Bergamo. I love that car.
Mechanic: I'll have to ask the curator.
Thank you.
Curator: I'll make an exception, but you can't go inside. I'll show you the back seat.

Thank you so much. I won't touch it. I just want to take some pictures.

What are these ropes on the top?

Curator: They were for inserting the flaps of the roof.

Wow! There's a drink cabinet. There's even a beauty case, and brushes for clothes. Everything about it is beautiful.

I see even the front seat is well furnished. What's that?

Curator: The windscreen wiper.

Yeah, sorry. Can we open the windscreen?

Curator: You could open them back then. They were very modern these cars. The only unreliable feature was the breaks. Very dangerous.

I see. You've been really kind. Thank you for letting me take photos. You've given me a real gift.

Curator: No problem. I must go now. They're expecting me.

Thank you.

I still can't fully digest what happened. I'll go and see the rest of the museum then come back here.

Rudolph, are you there?

Oops, there's someone here.

I'll get back to you later.

Cool, there are some movie cameras and gramophones. I'll check out the cameras first.

Oh lord, I can see your reflection on the glass!

Warn me next time.

Rudolph: Sorry. I can't exactly show myself.

I understand, but I could get a heart attack!

Rudolph: Look, we used this to shoot my movies. Memories...

Do you miss them?

Rudolph: A little.

Don't be like that. Tell me more.

Rudolph: Are you trying to distract me?

Yes. I hate seeing you sad.

Rudolph: Check out this video camera. We used it for The Eagle.

I've seen that movie many times. I love it so much.

You're so charming to the Tsaritsa. Your imitation of a French teacher using his hands to mime the mask of Black Eagle the bandit was beyond elegant.

Show me how it's done.

Rudolph: Do I have to?

Yes, please, come on.

Fantastic! You've got real class.

Obviously second nature for you.

How I wish the others could see you. Or maybe not...

I know. This section makes you nervous.

Come on. Let's see the bicycle and motorbikes.

Did you have a motorbike?

Rudolph: No, but I had a bicycle in Italy. You know that I prefer cars.

Yes, we'll go back and see them later.

Amazing, the bikes look like ours! Look at that 1924 motorbike. If it weren't for the brakes and seat, you'd think it was from to-day.

Rudolph: I don't know whether to take that as a compliment or a reference to how old I am.

The first. After all, a lot of things I take for granted were invented by your generation.

Rudolph: I like computers though. They can do anything.

True, but would you trade your time for mine?

Rudolph: What a dumb question. I'm obviously attached to what I know.

They're staring at me. They see me talking to myself. I'll put a headphone on, and pretend I'm on the phone.

Rudolph: In my days, you'd already be in a straightjacket.

In mine too, or at least forced to make a few visits to the psychiatrist.

What's so funny?

Rudolph: I liked that joke.

Yours are funnier.

In case you don't know, I think you're really sweet. A touch too insistent with your perfectionism though. There were times when you pushed me out of bed to get to the exercise bike in which I'd have killed you.

Oh, sorry. It's a figure of speech.

But you're my best friend. I really like you, and don't think I could manage without you.

I'd feel lost without you, like a Borg outside the collective.

Rudolph: What the hell's a Borg?

Sorry, of course you don't know. There's a science fiction series called *Star Trek*, which is set in the future and features characters from other planets. Some of them get kidnapped and have mechanical parts attached to them. All Borg are part of a collective, connected to each other via a hive mind. They're never alone, and their thoughts are linked.

Rudolph: I see. In the same way ours are?

That's right. I mean, I'm used to it that I can no longer stand the silence in my head.

Rudolph: Look at those funny typewriters.

You're right! The keys are on the sides.

Rudolph: Wow, I wasn't even born when they were invented!

Feeling young? You've finally found something from the past you've never seen.

Rudolph: You could say that.

Shall we look at the Isotta? This one's superb. When it came out, I'd been dead for three years.

If you'd been alive, you'd have started an Isotta collection.

Rudolph: Did you know that I had three cars.

Yes.

Rudolph: What's this, a catalogue? Like the ones in the magazines?

More or less.

Rudolph: Do they still keep newspapers in the libraries?

Yes, but not paper ones.

Rudolph: Of course. You have computers now.

Yep.

Just look at how marvelous the Isotta is.

Rudolph: I'd like to take it for a spin and drive around the countryside with you.

If only!
You'd be in the driver's seat though. It can't have been easy to maneuver.
Rudolph: It's a question of habit. The roads were hellish even in my day. Los Angeles was teaming with cars, and the cops were waiting at every crossroad. Some however had traffic lights installed. The road regulations weren't so strict. Now you've got tons of signs and rules. I'd never be able to memorize them all.
They're necessary now, seeing as there are more cars.
Rudolph: Let's check out the stuff from my days.
Sure.
Where are you?
You've vanished.
Hi Alessandra. I'm done here. We can go if you like.
Rudolph: Sorry, the nostalgia got to me. See you at home. I'd like to be alone for now.

September 5 2014

It's been days since I last saw Rudolph. He says he's been feeling sad since the trip to the museum.
I knew I'd miss him, but not this much.
Rudolph: Forgive me.
Hi Rudolph. Where were you? I was worried!
Rudolph: Why?
I was afraid I'd never see you again.
Rudolph: That will never happen. Don't worry.
Don't worry indeed! I never know where you are when I can't see you. But that's not the issue here. What bothers me is that you could tire of me one day.
Rudolph: I'm not the easily bored one here, am I?
True, it can happen that I need to try out new things, but feelings are completely different.
Anyway, aren't you my favorite ghost? You always say so yourself!
Rudolph: Sorry, I hadn't noticed this before, but I'm actually slightly happy that you missed me so much. Come here, give me

a hug. I've wanted this so much. The sex is fine, but it's the sweetness I love most.
I could switch preferences of course. It depends on my mood.
I don't know where you come from. Your feelings and perceptions seem as real as those of a living person. Maybe that's the novelty I like about you. Don't worry, I won't get bored of you.
Rudolph: I sometimes get scared, because I think about how you can sense my emotions. I hope you'll never know what I really think.
Emotions come from the soul. They're very revealing, and it's people like me who can perceive them. Thoughts on the other hand are more reserved. They don't brim with sensations like pleasure or sadness. They're difficult to figure out.
Rudolph: Can you touch my face? I like it when you do it.
Thank you. It's the little moments like these which I find most rewarding. I've brought you a gift.
Wow. What is it? I'm curious.
Rudolph: What is it?! Look carefully.
I don't know!
Rudolph: It's my mother's cameo. I managed to find it. I want you to have it.
Can I keep it in my bag?
Rudolph: Sure. The important thing is that it's always with you.
That's very kind of you. Thanks.
Rudolph: Will you give me something special for my birthday?
Like what? You know I'm not exactly loaded.
Rudolph: I was thinking of something special which money can't buy.
Alright, I'll give it some thought.
I'm off, but don't disappear! You promised.
Rudolph: Where do you think you're going? Kiss me first, then go.
Of course. You've no idea how much I've wanted to.
Till later.

Hello world! Morning Rudolph!
What a beautiful day.
Rudolph: Why do you think that is?
You know perfectly well!
Rudolph: Are you implying that I woke you up last night for a bout of "impetuous" sex?
No idea. I don't remember.
Stop tickling me. Stop it, I can't take it. Alright, yes, someone woke me.
Rudolph: Then what?
I can't talk this way, stop it, please. You know I can't talk when you tickle me there.
Yes, I got woken up for "impetuous" sex.
Rudolph: Who by?
A sexpot. Handsome, smart, cultured, talented, and very...
Rudolph: Very what?
I'm recording this. It's a little naughty.
Rudolph: Shall I say it?
No! Let's just say "involved".
Rudolph: If you say so.
You have a lovely laugh.
Rudolph: We both do.
When you say these things, you don't sound melodramatic at all.
And you say it in such a manly way. Determined, deadpan.
I'm madly in love. I need some air! There, that's better.
I've got a lot to do today. Will you stay with me?
Rudolph: Don't I always?
Yes, but put some extra effort today.
Wait, don't say anything. The exercise bike! You don't need to force me today or drag me by my hair. I'll go myself!

Every day I feel happier, and I ask myself how it is possible. His presence, his way of loving me, both make me feel alive. I so want to continue this experience called life.

May 1 2015

It's been a while, and life has hit me hard. A person close to me has had cancer. It one of those requiring multiple organ removals, though there is still a chance to survive. It was the most difficult period in my life. Rudolph always stood by me. He helped me keep awake whilst I drove exhausted. He assured me everything would go well. He kept me lucid in the most difficult times. I've recently come to know two very special people at the hospital, both called Maria.
The first is a perfect wife and mother; she's so sweet and I've grown to love her. The second is a literature teacher. She's very beautiful and I've enjoyed exchanging laughs with her, despite her surgery. I miss her. I love you both. Who knows if I'll see them again? That's what money's for.
I know that the cancer treatment center isn't the best place to relax, but the balcony and chapel have been places of profound peace for me.
We're back home now, and I hope things will return to normal soon. Obviously, Rudolph and I haven't been very affectionate with each other in this period.
I miss him. I want him to hold me!
I'm tired, so tired. Although I keep my smile on, this hurdle's been a hard one to overcome. I don't know how I'd have managed if Rudolph wasn't here to support me.
Thank you, my love.

It's one of those days. I really miss having non-stop sex and the desire we both had for each other, the feeling of being constantly aroused, even when we couldn't see each other, his hands working under my clothes as I spoke to people, unaware of what was going on.
I want his body and I miss his desire for me.
I can't take it anymore. I need to see him.
I want you, Rudolph. I've never longed for anyone else. I love everything about you.
Please, make yourself visible again. I'm losing my mind. I need to make love to you.

It's almost Rudolph's birthday, his 120th to be exact! I have no idea what gift that money can't buy I could give him.
Hi Rudolph! Nice to see you again! You can't imagine how I've longed for this moment. Please, hug me. Did you read what I wrote yesterday?
Rudolph: Come here my love. I want to hold you in my arms. I've missed you too. Why are you crying?
Because I am happy. I know you hadn't abandoned me, but I wanted to see you. Now that you're here, I can barely hold back my tears.
Let me touch you, squeeze you. How wonderful it is to hold you tight. We must never part again, no matter what. Promise me.
Rudolph: I promise.
I've been thinking that it's going to be difficult to find a good present for you.
Rudolph: I need you to do something for me.
What?
Rudolph: You know antibiotics?
Of course, why?
Rudolph: I need you to get two boxes of them. I need them.

It's been a while since we've met, and now you're asking for such absurd things. What does a dead man need with antibiotics!

Rudolph: A friend of mine is very ill, and he has no way of getting any medication.

Where does he live? Why can't he get to them himself?

Rudolph: You're asking too many questions.

That is one of the presents I ask of you.

But I'll have to spend money.

Rudolph: It's not the actual present, but it will help me get to it.

What you ask isn't that simple. I've got some pharmacist friends. I'll ask them.

Wouldn't you like something a bit more immediate, from me? Why are you shaking your head?

Rudolph: Something's wrong, but I can't talk about it. I know we haven't met in a long time, but what I have in mind is so special that everything else doesn't matter anymore. Tell me you'll be mine forever.

You're acting strangely. It's as if you're afraid of something.

Rudolph: You're right, but let's talk about something else.

Tell me something about the twenties.

Rudolph: My Isotta was fantastic. I raised a few eyebrows driving it around the city. An unforgettable experience. Where's the pin I gave you?

In my purse.

Why are you rummaging through it?

Rudolph: I saw someone yesterday drop a note in it. Don't look at me like that, it's true!

Go ahead and look. You're wrong.

You know my heart beats only for you.

Rudolph: If it beat for anyone else, I'd stop it.

What's all this! You'd never hurt me.

Rudolph: Forgive me, you're right.

Stop it! Put the pillow down. I'm not in the mood.

God, you're boring. I don't see you for ages, and all you can be is an absolute bore. Come on, defend yourself! What, are you a wimp?

Rudolph: Stop it, or I won't answer for my actions.
Is that what you want?
There, you can't move anymore. See what a manly ghost can do?
You talk too much. Why don't you do something for once?
Rudolph: Of course. I love you.

May 4 2015

You're splendid, Rudolph!
I forgot just how handsome you are, and how good making love to you is. Let me look at every inch of you. Shall we make up for lost time?
Rudolph: No, let's go and check out another Isotta Fraschini.
Where?
Rudolph: Let's go to the Vittoriale, the shrine of Italian victories. A friend of mine is there.
You mean D'Annunzio?
Rudolph: Yes, I met him in Rome. Another splendid specimen of the Italian male.
Alright, let me get set.
Rudolph: Put something sexy on.
Why?
Rudolph: I can't tell you.
Get a tight red dress and some high heels.
Aren't they a bit impractical?
Rudolph: Don't worry, bring some walking shoes for when we go through the gardens.
Yes sir! Whatever you say. Let's get back on topic when we return though.
Rudolph: I never said we'd leave it.
Say no more.
Rudolph: Aren't you going to turn off the microphone?
I like re-listening to you.
Rudolph: I liked it when we sang a few minutes ago.
You sing really well. I haven't found a single thing other than cooking that you can't do.

Rudolph: Knitting.
Shut up!
Rudolph: I can't even make a sweatshirt.
Oh let's go, you big baby.
Rudolph: You sure about that?
Oh stop it! Let's go.
Rudolph: Don't forget to bring some water. It's a long trip.
Hey, hands off! You slapped me too hard.
I must say, that's one hell of a tush you have.
Rudolph: Let's get moving! Here's how things stand.
You know you drive well.
More or less.
Rudolph: When are you going to learn to accept compliments every now and then? Aren't you a Gemini? You should be a narcissist.
Must be the ascendant Scorpio influence.
Rudolph: That's a good ascendant. Fits perfectly with a Taurus.
I'm no expert.
Rudolph: Both signs like making love to each other.
Stop! Let's put some music on and sing.
Rudolph: Good idea. Put "Même si" on.
Sure thing!
I like your French accent.
Rudolph: Blame my mother.
And the rest of the blame should go to your father, I imagine.
The other day I told a friend of mine that the best-looking cooking students I encountered during my travelling days came from Taranto. What say you?
Rudolph: I agree.
It was hard explaining everything all day, but the company of the students was nice.
Taormina is an unforgettable place I visited during my travels. Sicilians are such a gallant people. Their respect for women is from another time.
Rudolph: Are they like me?
Exactly the same.

I enjoyed visiting the hotels. They were so well maintained. It was one of the best times of my life.
Rudolph: What about now?
Jealous?
Rudolph: It would be nice if you came out and said that nothing compares to what you're living through right now.
They obligate their women to drive.
Rudolph: Are you changing subject on me?
Yes!
But you're right. It's the most beautiful period of my life and, before you ask me, I owe it to you.
Rudolph: That's better.
Are we there yet?
I don't know.
Rudolph: There's a sign!
Well done.
Rudolph: Thanks.
Here we are.
Let's park and find the entrance.
What a line!
Cashier: Yes?
One ticket, please.
Excuse me, which way is it to the Isotta Fraschini?
Cashier: Sorry, it's been loaned to some exhibition.
I don't believe it! Sorry, but I really wanted to see it.
Bye.
Dammit, just our luck!
D'Annunzio had good taste too. His villa should be amazing.
Rudolph: Who else do you know like that?
I don't remember...
The rooms are classy and full of trinkets, but they're a bit dark. The new part he was furnishing before dying is really bright though.
Rudolph: You're always avoiding my questions.
For God's sake, get off me. We're lucky no one's around. You made me jump when you touched my lower back.
Rudolph: Wasn't me.

Oh, so it was me then.
Rudolph: I swear it wasn't me!
Who was it then?
Rudolph: Guess.
Many women visiting here have had the same feeling.
I wouldn't call it a feeling.
Was it D'Annunzio? It can't be.
Rudolph: Believe it! Have you ever read The Child of Pleasure?
No.
Rudolph: Read it and you'll understand.
Let's go see the plane and hope nothing else happens.
Can't you make yourself visible? I want to hold your hand.
Rudolph: Here I am!
Thank you.
What are you doing? Put me down!
Rudolph: I'll carry you to the gardens on my shoulders.
Everyone's staring.
Rudolph: Good.
Put me down!
Rudolph: Didn't you want a bit of normality?
You call this normality? We're in a public space.
Rudolph: So what? Remember your objective: letting go. I'm carrying you because you'd stumble on those high heels.
That's very thoughtful of you, but I brought my normal shoes in my bag, just as you told me to.
Wait, let me kiss you...
It always feels like it's the first time.
You're so beautiful.
Rudolph: Let me introduce you to someone in these gardens. Change your shoes and follow me.
This park is wonderful. The stream's nice too. It's all so peaceful.
Rudolph: Watch out! You almost fell there.
Lucky for me, you were there to catch me.
Rudolph: I need to present the person I've been talking about to you.
You mean the man between the two trees?
Rudolph: Yes. He's agreed to meet you.

With pleasure then. I'm honored.

He's dressed funny.

Rudolph: You mean the white tunic?

Yes.

Rudolph: He's my teacher.

I don't get it.

What did he teach you? And what's the connection between the two of you? And by extension, me?

Rudolph: All in good time. I'll explain.

Is he a ghost?

Rudolph: Please, stop using that word! He's a friend. He showed me the way through many paths.

And yet he couldn't tell you of the danger you were in in 1926?

Rudolph: That's not how it works. It's more complicated than you realize.

Alright, I give up. Tell me everything.

Rudolph: He showed me how to manifest myself, and now he'll help you.

You were an actor. I'm no actress. I don't have the looks.

Rudolph: You talk way too much. You don't shut up for one minute when you're nervous.

You're right there.

Rudolph: You're not bad, but that's not what I meant. I was talking about the book.

Right, I hadn't thought of that. I don't think anyone will read it though.

I just write it because I want to reread the adventures we had together and have a laugh.

Rudolph: Don't you think someone else might like it?

I don't know. Fiorella's one friend I've read it to, and she likes it. She's a lot like me, a bit weird. She's nice.

She prayed a lot for me and my husband during the hard times. It was during that time that I worked out who my real friends were. She was among them. The others just ran off. They cancelled appointments, sometimes minutes before the established time.

It doesn't bother me too much, but I don't class their behavior as exactly stellar.

You, on the other hand, are my inseparable friend.

Rudolph: Not a bad moniker, though I'd prefer another.

How should I act with this gentleman?

Rudolph: Don't worry, let him sort it out.

Can he talk?

Rudolph: Be quiet. Just listen.

I can't hear anything, even in this silence.

Rudolph: Quiet.

Okay.

I feel like I'm floating. I'm not scared at all. I feel relaxed.

I just want to write, describe all my feelings and put them on the computer. For now I'll just use the Microphone.

Where's he gone?

Rudolph: He'll be back. He'll help you, just as he is doing with me.

Why? What can he do for you?

Rudolph: More than you think.

Alright, it's on a need to know basis.

Rudolph: You got it!

How boring.

Rudolph: Give me your hand. Let's go see D'Annunzio's grave.

May 4 2015, 11:00 am

Rudolph, slow down! Remember I'm asthmatic.

Rudolph: Weren't you getting better?

Yes, but not cured!

Rudolph: We'll need to work on your cardio.

Why? It's not like I'm going to sign up for the Olympics!

Rudolph: Not exactly.

Has it got something to do with sex?

Rudolph: Believe it or not, that isn't what I always think about.

Should I stop prying?

Rudolph: Please!

Let's go. All this mystery's a bore for someone inquisitive like me.

Rudolph: Fancy an ice cream? There's a stall over there.

Alright.

Bribed with an ice cream.

Rudolph: How is it?

Nice. Look, chocolate. Doesn't it bother you to look at it?

Rudolph: A little. You enjoy making me suffer, don't you, you little tease!

Remember how I was suffering before I met you?

I thought I was going crazy because I knew you were there, but I couldn't see you.

Rudolph: It wasn't my decision!

Alright, you're excused. Whose decision was it then?

Rudolph: Would you like to go to a restaurant later?

There! Why don't we?

Why is that lady staring at you like that?

Rudolph: Beats me.

Lady: Excuse me for staring, but you look like Rudolph Valentino, an actor from years back. Have you ever heard of him?

Rudolph: Yes, I've heard of him. I know he was a great performer. Handsome, smart, classy.

Lady: I see you know him well.

Rudolph: Yes, he had some real talent as an actor.

Lady: He was so handsome too. Don't get me wrong, but you look so similar to him. No offence, but he was the more handsome one.

Rudolph: Thank you, I'll take that as a compliment, miss...?

Lady: Ada.

Rudolph: Thanks again Miss Ada. It's been a pleasure.

Ada: Gosh, you kissed my hand!

Rudolph: I'm in character. Have a nice day.

Ada: Thanks, and to you and your friend.

Rudolph: She's my girlfriend.

I don't believe it. She recognized you.

I thought you'd been forgotten, your appearance at least.

But she said you're uglier than Rudolph Valentino.

Cat got your tongue? Still blushing?

Rudolph: Let's just say it was a nice experience.

Soaking it up, aren't we?

Rudolph: Pardon?

You're feeling all important now.

Rudolph: Indeed. Let me bathe in it some more!

So I'm your girlfriend now.

Rudolph: I didn't want her to think we were just friends.

Alright, that's enough.

Let's go to the restaurant.

Rudolph: I just wanted her to know that you're my girl. Isn't that how you'd put it?

Sure. Let's go.

Rudolph: What will you order?

You!

Rudolph: Very funny!

I'll need to check the menu, but I think I'll go for a salad. You know I never eat ham or meat dishes.

Rudolph: Indeed. You've got the means, but not the know-how.

Now who's being funny?

Hey, don't slap my ass!

Rudolph: That'll teach you.

It's a shame you won't be able to dine with me.

Rudolph: That's depressing. I'd like to do things that are impossible for me now.

Don't talk like that. I'll eat, and you'll go on a diet.

Rudolph: That was actually funny.

You're so sweet when you smile.

I love you!

Hey, are you crying?

Rudolph: Look how magnificent that horse is.

I didn't think there'd be any here.

Rudolph: What's with all the smiling?

It's funny how we keep changing subject.

Rudolph: Did it work this time?

It did.

You're staring at me a little too intensely.

Why are you squeezing my hand like that?

Rudolph: Is that a crime?

No, but it's a little embarrassing.

I'm not saying it's wrong, it's just that I'm not just some painting to be examined.

Rudolph: Thank God!

What I mean is, these days it's not normal to stare at a woman that way. You look a little crazy.

Don't laugh.

Ah, here's the salad.

Rudolph, stop looking at me eat!

Rudolph: But I do it all the time!

Yeah, but I can't see you.

Rudolph: Right. I'll just look around me then.

You're so childish!

Rudolph: Wasn't I a pig earlier?

Don't shout!

You shouldn't say things like that.

Rudolph: I don't get it. You people swear all the time, yet I can't say "pig"? You're always saying it!

Swear words are okay, even though they're rude. I only say "pig" in private.

Rudolph: That's absurd. Swear words yes, but "pig's" out.

You guys are weird.

So how should I behave?

Good question. I have no idea.

I think you should avoid making sexual references in public.

Rudolph: But you're always using that word referring to a certain intimate activity!

Swear words yes, sexual references no.

Rudolph: Unbelievable...

You act like pigs in bed, but aren't open about it, yet you openly swear like sailors.

I don't understand you people.

Just accept it.

I'll take another bite then let's go to the souvenir store. Let's see if they have a little Isotta Fraschini replica.

Look at this model. Isn't it wonderful?

It's a plane from the early 1900s.

Rudolph: I'm familiar with it.

When will you tell me more about your life?

Rudolph: Whenever you please, though I'd prefer it if you didn't write about it.

Why?

Rudolph: If you don't mind, I'd like to maintain an air of mystery around me.

Is it true that you knew Charlie Chaplin?

Rudolph: Sure. We were friends, and we used to dine together a lot. There's even a photo of us at the Ambassador Hotel in Los Angeles.

I'll look for it.

It's a beautiful hotel. I'd love to spend a night there, assuming it still exists.

Rudolph: Maybe you will when you're done writing and go on a book signing tour in LA.

You have such faith in me!

Rudolph: Trust me. I'm one of your readers. Everyone will like it and you'll sleep in my house, or what's left of it.

Stop it. You're getting my hopes up.

I don't want to be famous anyway.

Rudolph: Who cares? Just write it for me then.

That's enough. We get too serious every time we talk about it.

Come on, let's get that plane. I really like it.

I'll take the red one. It's your favorite color after all.

Too bad about the Isotta. It's not our day today.

Rudolph: Shall we go to the lake now?

Why?

Rudolph: I miss the water.

Will you remain visible and not disappear?

Rudolph: It can be done.

Rudolph, where are you?

There you are! I thought you pulled one of your tricks again.

Rudolph: I'd just gone to see the horizon over the road. Nice place this Gabriele.

Come on, let's go to the lake!

Rudolph: Get that book done. I want you to come with me.

What if your fangirls built a shrine for you in Los Angeles?

Rudolph: I don't need one.

Right, but it would be cute!

Rudolph: Trust me, I don't need one.

Alright, never mind.

Here we are! The lake.

Rudolph: Wanna go skinny dipping?

Are you crazy? Look at all the people here.

Oh my God, what are you doing?

Stop it!

Rudolph: Come in, the water's great.

I think not!

Rudolph: Do I have to drag you in?

No, stay there. I'll throw you your underwear.

You could make an effort in buying more modern-looking pants you know!

Come closer. I'll just put my feet in.

No, I'm still dressed!

Great, now I'm soaked. What now?

Rudolph: I'm happy.

Am I allowed to say that in public?

You're butt-naked in a lake. I don't think it really matters what you say.

Rudolph: I agree.

Hand me my fabulous underwear.

Do you think they noticed my wiener?

They'd have to be blind not to.

Rudolph: I'll give you that.

There, it's covered now. Jealous?

Jealous of what?

Rudolph: That other women have seen me in the nude.

Can we change subject please?

At least it's nice and warm today.

Let's get dry and go home. I think we've exhibited enough of ourselves for one day.

Stop giggling and get in the car!
The way back's long. Let's put some music on.
Rudolph: I need to pee!
We'll stop at a service station, okay?
Rudolph: No way!
What's with that face?
Something wrong?
I'll stop.
Rudolph, stop staring at me.
Did you hear me?
Stop laughing!
Ah, right. I forgot you don't have that function.
I must be out of my mind.
Hilarious...
Ah, we've arrived!
What a beautiful day. It's been a while since I've felt so relaxed.
I feel at peace.
I wish this day would never end.
Rudolph: Guess what's up next!
What, here?
Rudolph: Are you ready to cry out with ecstasy and go crazy, apparently all alone in the car?
Dumb question.
Rudolph: Wow, what a mess. You've really let yourself go. Open your eyes and let's go. Everyone outside the car's staring.
Oh my!
Oops.
Sorry, I was rehearsing a part I need to play for a show. How was it?
Observers: Swell. You'll be a real hit!
Thanks a lot.
Good day to you.
Observers: Where will the show be?
At Milan. I'm still auditioning though.
Observers: Just do what you did now. There's no way they'll reject you.
Thanks again.

That was really embarrassing, Rudolph.
Rudolph: I've never laughed so much.
You'll be paying for the ticket.
Let's go.

May 6 2015

Happy birthday!
Where are you?
It's your 120th!
Where've you gone?
I don't have your present, but I'd still like to wish you a happy birthday.
I feel dumb shouting around the house like this. Where are you?
He's gone!
Not again! I'm calling Fiorella. She'll take my mind off it.
Hi Fiorella. How's Gedeone?
Fiorella: Alright. He's gone and done it again. You should know he's a real pesky cat. Just today he ripped up a roll of paper I needed.
I know. Pets take on the personalities of their owners.
Fiorella: You're right there.
I'll be around your neck of the woods tomorrow. I'm going hiking with my brother. Wanna come? You'll finally get to know him.
Yeah, I'll be around, but I'd also like to see Gedeone.
Fiorella: I'm not putting him in the car. He'd dig his claws in the upholstery. It would be like having a bouncing furball in the vehicle.
I get it. I'll pop in the next time I pass Varese.
Fiorella: Yeah, it's better that way. Till later. I need to go, there's a call coming from my lawyer.
Alright. See you tomorrow.
I'll distract myself if work. I doubt he'll come today.

May 13 2015

Cooking class today!

Pizza and focaccia. Too bad I'm allergic to yeast.

I'll try the Genoese focaccia, I just can't resist. Nobody touches my Genoese focaccia!

Same old: tidy the school, prepare documentation, the certificates and do some shopping. Couldn't my mom have spared me the allergy? I can't even approach a dusty surface without a breathing mask.

There!

Now for some coffee.

Coffee with cream.

I've written a poem all about it, dedicated to Gianluca. He likes this drink too. Remember that!

Here it is:

CREAM – DEDICATED TO GIANLUCA
AS WHITE AS SNOW,
AS LIGHT AS A CLOUD,
AS SWEET AS A BABY'S KISS,
AS SOFT AS A DREAM,
I WATCH YOU IN ECSTASY AND YOU MELT ON MY LIPS.

Yum! Just reading it makes me hungry.

I'm alone, but I'm happy.

Man, these ghosts are such teases.

Bah!

Tomorrow I'll go out for coffee with Fiorella. She hasn't dropped by yet, owing to some problem with the doctor. Just another one of Fio's usual debacles.

I always abbreviate names, as I'm always in a hurry. Fiorella, therefore, has become Fio, Debora Deb, while I address my husband by his surname.

Why? It's a long story. Maybe another time.

May 14 2015

Hi Fio.
How's it going?
Fiorella: Okay. You free?
Sure, just let me inform my husband. Let's do some shopping and grab a coffee.
Fiorella: Sounds like a plan!
Tight clothes?
Fiorella: Yep.
I've added you to the book I'm writing.
I'll put this conversation in it. You don't mind if I continue recording?
Fiorella: Go ahead.
Let's have coffee later. I first need to show you a dress.
Have you seen one like this before? It's a little weird.
The one next to it isn't bad. Cut the mike, I can't have the rest of what I want to say recorded.
Alright, let's paint the town red. It's off!

May 27 2015

Same old, same old.
Thank God for the classes. I love fooling around with the students. I count some of them as real friends.
The rest however...
Not a peep.
He's gone!
It's my birthday tomorrow, and he's nowhere to be seen.
Won't he leave me a present of some kind at least?

May 28 2015

I've had a wonderful dream.
I was heading to Los Angeles for a book presentation.
I wanted to walk through the city where Rudolph had lived. I didn't know him in the dream. I'd done my research and knew

80

pretty much everything about 1920s Los Angeles, but nothing about it as it is today. I hoped that some of the places he'd lived in were still around. I'd agreed on the long trip on condition that I got to sleep in "Rodolfo Valentino"'s house, or at least what's left of it. I arrived at the Falcon Lair with an interpreter. We asked to see the city skyline.

I'd finally arrived alone at his house. LA had certainly changed since his death, but at least I was there. What could be more exciting? Even though it didn't look the way it did in the book, it seemed like he could be there with me. Only death separated us, until he took me in his arms. I didn't see him, because he was behind me. I was indescribably happy. Teats ran down my cheeks. I couldn't stop crying with joy. I only had fifteen minutes before the guide came to fetch me, but I squeezed his hands, hoping he'd never leave me. I pondered over how I wanted time to stop. I even took pleasure in hearing his voice.

He asked if I liked what I could see. It was the first time I could hear it. How could I describe such a heavenly feeling?

His hands were marvelous. When he grabbed my arm and turned me towards him, I melted. It was beautiful, classy even.

He wasn't dressed as he was in the book. He wore an elegant brown suit. Splendid! I was listening to Ed Sheeran's "Photograph" on my MP3 player when he wrapped his arm around my waist and began doing a slow dance. I didn't hesitate. I joined in his movements. I couldn't be more in love. I'm awake now. I hope this dream becomes a reality. I want to experience those emotions again.

Come back to me! I love you!

May 30 2015

I'm furious. He's not getting away with it this time.
There are no excuses anymore. He hasn't shown up in ages.
Enough's enough. He can go screw himself!
I'm sick of him, and he has the gall to talk about commitment.
If he's cheating on me, I'll smack him so hard, no matter who it's with!

Rudolph: Touchy touchy.
Show yourself, and I'll show you just how touchy I can be.
Rudolph: Happy birthday!
Forget it. It was the day before yesterday anyway.
Rudolph: I know.
I'm glad you do.
I was hoping you'd show up.
You're always harping on about your know-how, your chivalry, your supposed understanding of women, yet you act with complete insensitivity. Any man could have done better!
Latin lover, my ass!
Rudolph: If I materialize, will you hit me?
Don't bother. I'm too ticked off right now.
Rudolph: What's all this? You sound like someone from my time.
You lie down with dogs, you get fleas.
Rudolph: Dogs?
It's a metaphor.
Rudolph: I'll be on my way.
Don't come back!

June 2 2015

The cooking classes are the best antidote.
They help get through hard times, and there've been plenty this semester.
They've been my salvation.
I'll never forget him. When I'm old and think back on this period with a smile, it will be because I'll remember the classes and the sense of peace they gave me.
You've all been fantastic.

June 5 2015

What makes us so anxious? What makes us lose sight of the positivity in our lives?
Hurrying.
Rushing prevents you from living in the now.

What's the point of running towards a goal you don't even care about?
As Rudolph says, you need to let go and live with no thought of the morrow.
I need to chill out and switch my mind off.

June 8 2015

I was sat in my armchair admiring the tree towering over my garden.
I perceived its might through the window, when suddenly some good memories came flashing back. I recalled the happiness I felt when dad took us to the Ticino River. We travelled long distances to find a local restaurant. How could I forget the fragrance of the food we'd ordered as I waited for it to be brought to the table? Or the sensation of running through the fields and jumping into the river? The feeling of grass under my bare feet as I ran towards the rocks separating me from the water?
The water was cool and shallow. It felt refreshing in the summer heatwave.
Peace, sunshine, water and lots of joy.
What happened to you, Rudolph?
What's with the Sheik costume?
You disappear for all this time and then reappear dressed like that and covered in makeup.
Rudolph: Sorry, I needed to see you and didn't have time to change.
What are you talking about?
Are you still acting?
Rudolph: Sorry, I didn't explain myself. Or perhaps I wanted to, but now's not the right time.
So, not only do you vanish, you come back looking like a lunatic.
What's wrong with you?
Rudolph: I can't answer that right now.
Where are you going?
I'm getting out of here. I'm tired of this.
Rudolph: Don't. Everything will become clear.

Everything?
Rudolph: Be patient. Everything will be better than you think.
Come here. I want to hold you. I've missed you so much.
I'll never leave you. That was the last time. I'm done now.
Dammit, there's still sand on my clothes!
Oh, I almost forgot. That was a beautiful dream you had on your
birthday! Come, let's dance to "Phograph". Put the gramophone
on, or whatever you call it these days.
I get what you mean, though an MP3 player hardly looks like a
gramophone. Anyway, both can make you dream whilst listening to music.
Rudolph: Have you heard my records?
I know people like them.
What's with the present tense?
Rudolph: Does it matter?
If it weren't for the fact that you're dead, I'd say you were drunk
or high on something.
Rudolph: Alright, let's dance.
I don't really feel like it.
Rudolph: I love the smell of your hair. Why are you dressed so
sexily?
I'm going out.
Rudolph: With who?
Friends.
Rudolph: If they're just friends, why are you dressed that way?
Change into something else!
No way.
Rudolph: Have I missed something? Did you start seeing another
man whilst I was gone?
Why are you looking at me like that? Are you going to say something unpleasant?
Yes, bye. They've arrived.
Rudolph: Please tell me nothing's changed.
Bye. Sorry, I really need to go. It's what you do with me all the
time in any case. The only difference is that you can see what I
get up to. I, on the other hand, could never see what you were
doing.

Bye.

June 9 2015

What the...?
What are you doing in my bed? Cover yourself!
Rudolph: Why? You've seen me naked before.
Go away!
Rudolph: Stop it.
Fifty Shades of Gray *my ass, let's do this.*
You expect me to just be compliant?
Rudolph: Come and look at me. Am I so ugly? Don't I excite you?
Give me your hand. Let me rub it on my chest.
Aw shoot... Don't go.
Mailman: Registered mail.
Not again. We've got the most zealous mailmen in all the country.
Just our luck.
Won't be long.
I had to pay a fine, obviously.
And now that I'm back, you've disappeared again.
Where are you?
Typical. Gone!
I'm ticked off again.

June 11 2015

Ow! What was that?
A rose? On my pillow?
There's a lily too.
This flower's so fragrant. I love it.
I don't know where you are, but thank you. Wait, to hell with that!
I can't take it anymore. I hate you.
Here's what you can do with your flowers.
There, gone!

I keep finding flowers everywhere I go, especially lilies.
Telephone: Hey, Marco here.
I know, I've memorized your number. How are you?
Marco: Okay. I'm in Italy for a month and thought I'd drop in. Is your husband there?
No, sorry. You know he's always out for work.
Marco: Still teaching in other schools?
Unfortunately yes. He's in Brussels now, teaching professionals.
Marco: That's a shame. I wanted to catch up with him.
You're not coming then?
Marco: Of course I am! Why don't we go to a restaurant at Treviglio? It even has a Michelin star.
Certainly! When? I'll need to know the exact day, as I'm busy with some new classes.
Marco: Friday, June 19 at half six.
That's perfect! I'm free on Friday. Let's meet at the school.
Marco: Call me if you have any problems.
There won't be any. We've got a lot to talk about. It's been one hell of a time here.
Marco: See you on the 19th.
Bye.
See you soon.
Rudolph: Who's Marco?
Oh, welcome back.
I see you still exist. I thought you'd vanished.
You remember me every now and then. Who am I to always intrude on your thoughts? I only wanted you to make up your mind over staying with me.
I'm just a hamster to you, a hamster you neglect and feed only when you're afraid it might die. You watch it in its cage, pet it a little then put it back in its pen, wondering why you bought it in the first place. But it's not a pair of shoes bought on impulse, and neither am I.
Anyway, Marco's a nice guy. He's a successful businessman and a great public speaker.

Rudolph: Sounds too nice for my tastes.
Is he attractive?
I can't deny he is. You'll see.
Rudolph: Why did you accept his invitation?
You're never here.
I've gone from the frying pan to the fire.
I've never been attracted to him. He's too serious and too much of a perfectionist. It's as if he's constantly trying to show people what he's made of. The typical attitude of someone with daddy issues.
Rudolph: So what's changed?
I want to get to know him better. It could be that he isn't what I always imagined him to be.
One of his Skype messages really got to me.
Rudolph: Now you're just being hurtful.
So are you every time you leave me alone.
You need to figure out how much you really care for me. Show me or we're done.
Rudolph: I'm sorry you've understood nothing about me, but most of all that you are unable to trust me.
I've put my trust in many, and for what?
I'm stuck here within these four walls not knowing what the future holds for me.
Rudolph: No one does.
You're totally clueless. You men are all the same, dead or alive. You just run away from everything.

June 19 2015

I can't wait to see Marco again.
I'll wear a classy skintight dress. I want to be admired, but not gawked at.
I'll put on my five inch heels. Marco's a tall man after all. He's got class and a nice body.
It's almost half six. Time to change.
I'm as nervous as a teenager. What a funny feeling.
There, done!

Yep, I'm ready now. I've put the microphone in the bag. Everything's set.
Here he comes.
Hey Marco. Looking smart today.
Marco: You too.
Let me lock up and I'm with you. Those flowers smell nice. Are they for me?
Marco: They are.
Thanks, I'll put them in the vase. I'll be with you in a second.
Marco: Okay.
Wow. What kind of car did you rent?
Marco: It's mine actually.
You have a Jaguar? It's my favorite kind. I've never been in one.
Marco: There's a first time for everything.
Well, actually my favorite is the 8A model Isotta Fraschini, but I don't know anyone who owns one. Jaguar's in second place though.
Marco: Not to blow my own trumpet here, but I know that model well. My father had one.
In that case, let me get my notebook. It has all of my poems, including one dedicated to the Isotta.
Marco: Shall we go?
Sure.
Could I see your father's Isotta.
Marco: I'll ask.
You've no idea how happy that'd make me.
Let's park near the bank. There's never any space around here.
Marco: I like this region. Very familiar. What are the locals like?
They're okay. I've got lots of friends who were born here. I could never leave.
Marco: Do you like warm areas?
Sure, a lot.
Marco: Wait here. I'll go in first.
Charming.
Marco: I do what I can!
Waiter: Do you have a reservation?
Marco: Yes. The name's G.

Waiter: Right this way. Here are your menus.
I hadn't thought of the cost. This restaurant's expensive.
Marco: So?
You offered to pay. I wouldn't want you to spend too much.
Marco: Don't worry about it.
What'll you order?
I'll take the plateau royal. I don't think I'd be able to manage anything else.
Marco: Perfect. We can share it, seeing as I like it too.
Can I show you my poems?
Marco: Of course.
Can I read them?
I'd like that.

INFINITY
I GATHERED WHAT LITTLE STRENGTH I HAD AND SEARCHED FOR LIFE.
I'VE FOUND LIFE THROUGH YOU AND HAVE TRIED TO KNOW YOU.
I KNOW YOU BUT I CAN'T SEE YOU, BECAUSE YOU DON'T BELONG HERE. YOU BELONG TO DEATH.

FREEDOM
RAGE DOMINATES MY THOUGHTS.
UNBEARABLE EMOTIONS CONSPIRE TO PUT AN END TO THESE MOMENTS.
I CAN'T TAKE THESE EVENTS ANYMORE.
I WANT EVERYTHING TO BE CONDENSED IN ONE SIMPLE BUT DEEP WORD:
FREEDOM.

MY LOVE
WE WALKED HAND IN HAND WHILST THE WORLD CANCELLED ITSELF OUT.
WE CLUNG ON TO OUR POINTLESS DREAMS AND OUR UNION.
WE RAN TO OUR FUTURE LIKE TWO YOUNGSTERS.
TWO YOUNGSTERS WHO DON'T FEAR TOMORROW.

THE DREAM THAT OUR HANDS WOULD NEVER LET GO OF EACH
OTHER.

LONLINESS
I CAN'T SENSE YOU ANYMORE.
I CAN'T SENSE YOUR LOVE ANYMORE.
I CAN'T SENSE THE DESIRE YOU HAVE FOR ME ANYMORE.
I DON'T KNOW WHAT'S HAPPENING.
I ASK MYSELF IF THIS IS THE END OF OUR ETERNAL LOVE.
HOW CAN A LIFE BE LIVED WITHOUT YOU?
MY GREATEST FEAR IS BEING ALONE.
ALONE IN A SOLITUDE WITHOUT YOU.

KABAR
I SMILE BECAUSE IT'S A WONDERFUL DAY.
I SMILE BECAUSE I FEEL ALIVE.
I SMILE BECAUSE LIFE IS BEAUTIFUL.
I SMILE BECAUSE YOUR EYES MEET MINE.
I SMILE BECAUSE YOU FOLLOW ME EVERYWHERE I GO.
I SMILE BECAUSE I CAN COUNT ON YOU ALWAYS.
I SMILE BECAUSE YOU'RE HAPPY, NO MATTER WHAT I DO.
I SMILE WHEN YOU TAP ME WITH YOUR TAIL.

DEATH
I DID AWAY WITH THE MEMORY OF PAIN,
I DID AWAY WITH THE PAIN IN MY HEART,
THE WORD LOVE WAS CARVED ONTO MY HEART SO OFTEN IT
NOW HURTS,
BUT I DIDN'T REALIZE YOU NO LONGER EXISTED.

THE SHEIK
AFTER A MILLION JOURNEYS ON YOUR COAST I DISEMBARKED,
FROM DISTANT LANDS I CAME,
ARRIVING WITH THE SURENESS OF EVERYTHING BEING POSSI-
BLE,
I TOILED IN A THOUSAND JOBS,
BUT FINALLY REACHED MY GOAL.

I DANCED AND PLAYED THE LOVERS' GAME.
I WAS LOVED,
BUT IT WASN'T REAL.
NOTHING WAS REAL.
DEATH WAS REAL.
TO HE WHO WHISKED ME AWAY LIKE SAND IN THE DESERT,
BLOT OUT THE SUN.

DESIRE
THANK YOU FOR HAVING CROSSED THE DISTANCE SEPARATING
US,
THANK YOU FOR HAVING FALLEN IN LOVE WITH ME,
THANK YOU FOR ALL THE TIMES I CAN FEEL YOUR PRESENCE,
THANK YOU FOR THE MOMENT IN WHICH WE CAN MEET.

CARION

UNITED IN A NEVERENDING DANCE,
A GRACEFUL, SINUOUS DANCE,
A DANCE FROM A BYGONE AGE,
WHERE EYES MEET
AND HANDS SQUEEZE.
NOTHING SEEMS TO STOP.
ONLY NOW DO I REALIZE THAT THIS SPELL
WILL END,
WILL END
INEXORABLY WHEN
THE BATTERY
RUNS LOW.

LOVE
I LOVE YOU,
I LOVE YOU FOR WHAT YOU ARE,
FOR THE INFINITY I SEE WITHIN YOUR EYES,
THE INFINITY I SENSE IN YOUR BREATH,
THE INFINITY I HEAR IN YOUR WORDS WHEN YOU SAY
I LOVE YOU.

FALCON LAIR
ENDLESS WAITING,
ENDLESS SACRIFICES
JUST TO SEE YOU.
MAJESTIC,
EVOCATIVE OF SPAIN,
IMMENSE GARDENS,
WITH YOU, THE HORIZON HAS NO BORDERS.
TAPESTRIES, SWORDS, MEMORIES OF A GLORIOUS PAST,
THE LIGHTNESS OF THE CLOTHS ADORNING THE ROOMS,
STRONG EMOTIONS HELD BACK.
AND NOW THAT CURIOUS ADMIRERS
GATHER BEFORE IT,
NOTHING REMAINS OF YOU
BUT A FEW ROOMS
IN MEMORY OF HE WHO'S PRAISES LOVE SANG.

DOUBT

I ALMOST FORGOT HOW.
THEN I LEARNED THAT PASSION WAS THE KEY
TO YOUR HEART.

8A ISOTTA FRASCHINI

I SEARCH FOR YOU,
I CRAVE YOU,
I DREAM OF YOU.
I WANT TO TRAVEL THE WORLD WITH YOU,
FEEL THE WIND IN MY HAIR.
WHERE ARE YOU?
I LOOK OUT FOR YOU
AND YOUR MULTICOLOURED SHINE.
MY EMOTIONS ARE HIGH.
I BRUSH AWAY A TEAR,
FOR I CAN FINALLY TOUCH YOU,
MY SHINY NEW 8A ISOTTA FRASCHINI.

NIGHT
I FEEL THE ECHO OF MY THOUGHTS,
I FEEL YOUR LIPS MOVE,
I FEEL THE CALM PERVADE MY EVERY CELL,
I FEEL MY FACE BRIGTHEN AT YOUR THOUGHT,
I FEEL A MEMORY FLOATING AWAY
IN NIGHT'S ABYSS.

NOW
IT'S TIME FOR EVERYTHING TO BE LAID BARE,
EVERY SENTENCE, WORD AND FEELING,
BEFORE YOU I WILL COME,
AND THE FACE OF LOVE I WILL DISCOVER.

CHOCOLATE
I SAW YOU LYING DOWN
ON A SOFT SHEET.
MY EYES SHONE,
MY HANDS WANTED TO TOUCH YOU.
I WANTED TO FEEL
THOSE EMOTIONS WHICH ONLY YOU CAN INSPIRE.
I WANTED TO PRESS MY LIPS TO YOU,
BITE YOU AND MAKE YOU MINE,
GET DRUNK ON YOU,
BE HAPPY WITH YOU,
DREAM WITH YOU,
BUT I CAN'T.
THE WARMTH YOU COULD GIVE ME
IS TOO MUCH.

WORD
FEELINGS,
DESIRES,
EMOTIONS,
ALL LOCKED WITHIN THIS WORD:
LOVE.

NATURE
I WAS WALKING BAREFOOT ON THE GRASS
TO MAINTAIN CONTACT WITH NATURE.
WHITE BUTTERFLIES FLUTTERED
LIGHTLY IN THE AIR.
THE SCENT OF FLOWERS CLOUDED MY MIND.
MY BREATHING SLOWED.
WITH EVERY STEP I REDISCOVERED
HOW MUCH MY WORRIES VANISHED.
ONLY DOWN DO I REALIZE THAT THERE'S NO BETTER WAY
TO REDISCOVER THE SILENCE OF INNER PEACE.

Marco: Is Kabar a dog or something?
Yes, the dog of Rudolph Valentino, an actor from the twenties.
Falcon Lair was his home.
Oh, and *The Sheik* is one of his movies.
Marco: I see you're something of a Valentino fangirl.
Yes.
Marco: I guess the Latin Lover has his charm.
Keep reading. I'd like you to finish before our orders arrive.
Marco: They're beautiful. I never took you for a poet.
Neither did I.
Marco: What do you mean?
They're just my way of expressing myself.
Marco: I can see that.
This dish is delightful, don't you think?
Sure, but isn't delightful an old-fashioned word? I'd expect you
to say "delicious".
Marco: What difference does it make?
None. It just reminded me of a friend.
Marco: Why do you suddenly become solemn when talking
about him?
He's something of a charmer.
Marco: As a friend?
Of course.
Let's change subject.
Marco: You said you've had a rough time.

Yes. Someone close to me got cancer.

It was devastating.

I convinced myself that, no matter how invasive the procedure would have been, everything would have turned for the better. This gave me the strength to keep working and find new material for the school.

Marco: Am I wrong in assuming that your husband was the one operated on?

Yes. Let's be open about it.

I like him a lot, and can't imagine life without him even though he's never here. The moment he comes back, he's off again on some tour.

Marco: You don't think he's cheating on you, do you?

I don't know. I don't want to think about it. I admit it's something I've thought about for years.

And how are you with women these days?

You're not married, are you?

Marco: No, but there's a lady I fancy.

Does she live near you?

Marco: No, she's in Italy.

I'm sorry to hear that. It must be hard.

Marco: It is, but mostly because she doesn't know how I feel about her.

Why not? Haven't you told her?

You're a polite and attractive guy. What couldn't she like about you?

Marco: I hope she thinks of me with similar enthusiasm.

Me too. You need to tell her.

Marco: I'll follow your advice.

Would you like to go somewhere else later?

There's a place called Bloom I've never been to. Wanna try?

Marco: Why not!

I wonder what people will think seeing me with you.

Marco: You've never been out with a friend before?

Not here.

Marco: I'll pay, then we'll head off.

Okay. I'll just go to the bathroom.

Marco: Let's find it with the satnav.
There it is.
It's really hot in here. Could you put the air conditioning on?
There's the sign for Bloom.
Nice, don't you think?
Marco: Sure. Let's go in.
Wow, there's a Charleston show today.
Did you know that I can dance it quite well?
Marco: Really? You're quite something.
Look at them go. They're so talented.
Marco: Come, let's sit at that table.
Your eyes are shining.
The dancers are just superb.
I'm not upset, just happy. There's no need to hold my hand.
Why are you staring at me like that? Something wrong?
What did you just do? You kissed me.
Marco: Sorry, I just lost myself there. I was just thinking about what you said.
Now the person I like knows.
Me?
Are you kidding?
You're the kind of man every woman wants.
You're perfect.
I've seen the way women look at you while listening to your public speeches.
Marco: There's a "but" coming, isn't there?
Yes, I love another. I totally love him, even if he's almost never here.
Marco: So there's no chance for me?
Not at the moment. Only if he keeps neglecting me.
I'm sorry if I've mislead you somehow.
Marco: I understand. Pity. Just know that I'll always be there for you.
Thank you. You're really special.
Marco: Not enough, apparently.
I think it's time you took me home.
Marco: Obviously. No sex then?

Excuse me?

Marco: Just breaking the tension. I wanted to leave you with a nice memory.

For a moment I thought you were serious. I'm happy to see this side of you.

Let's go.

It's been a nice evening, and I'll recall it with pleasure.

It's nice to know you're wanted.

Before you go, let me tell you this: your lips are fantastic.

Marco: You haven't seen the rest of me!

Silly!

Let's keep in touch.

Bye.

Marco: Bye.

June 20 2015

We women can be strange sometimes. Marco has everything. How could I reject him? Instead I'm staying with a husband who doesn't love me and, what's more, I'm having an affair with a man who doesn't exist. How could this be anymore stupid or absurd? I'm calling Marco. I can't continue this way.

Rudolph: Put the phone down!

Look who's back from the grave.

Sorry, poor choice of words.

Rudolph: I'm seriously ticked off right now. He kissed you!

And you let him touch you.

Are you done?

Rudolph: Stop throwing things at me. You could hurt me.

If that were true, this would be the appetizer of a three-course meal.

Rudolph: It's a little early for dinner.

Stop it!

What do you want from me?

Let's call it quits, Rudolph. My life's complicated enough as it is. I want things to be normal again, and I'd like to get to know Marco better.

Rudolph: You will do no such thing.

Do you even know how long it's been since you last touched me? How long I've been waiting for just one hour with you?

Please, if you love me, then just go. I can't take this anymore.

Rudolph: I love you too much to do that. Tomorrow, all of this will just be memory. Go to sleep, my love. Tomorrow will be a great day.

For what?

Rudolph: Can I hold you in my arms?

I'm going to regret this, but all right.

Why can't things be simpler? Why have you come?

Rudolph: Sleep, my love. Sleep.

30 June …. 8:00 am

Something smells different. It's sea air. How is that possible? I live near the plains. They can smell pungent at times, but never like this.

I open my eyes, but I don't recognize this place. What's going on?

Maybe I'm not truly awake yet, but this feels so real.

My God, now I see. I'm at your house. How is this possible? I don't…

Your house was demolished. How did you rebuild it?

Rudolph: Good morning.

Explain!

Rudolph: Don't shout, or the butlers will come running.

Who?

Rudolph: Where do you think you are?

At your place?

Rudolph: Correct.

Where are you taking me?

Rudolph: Look out of the window.

It's an Isotta Fraschini. Where did you find it?

Rudolph: It's mine.

Yours? I thought your cars were now in Switzerland.

Rudolph: Not yet.

Look closer.
I see a girl. She's wearing something straight from the twenties. Where did you find her?
Rudolph: At Sunset Boulevard.
Is this Los Angeles?
Rudolph: It is.
How is this possible? How can your house still be intact?
Rudolph: Look at me. Do you trust me?
Yes.
Rudolph: Wear these.
Where did you find them? They look genuine.
This dress is lovely.
Even the shoes look vintage.
I suppose they're back in fashion. These Cuban heels are great. I didn't know they could be so comfortable.
I like them.
Weren't the twenties fantastic! How do I look?
Rudolph: Sweet. Try putting your hair up a little. May I?
Sure.
Wear something vintage yourself. It'll be like we're really there.
Will you be invisible?
Rudolph: You can't imagine for how long.
You look just like a lady from my days.
Can you tell me where we are? Is this place some reproduction for a movie set in the twenties?
Rudolph: Come, let me show you my garden.
Those are the trees you imported from Italy. Every detail is exact.
I just saw the fountain.
That one at least still exists.
It's just as it was.
The set designers have done a really neat job. It all looks like what I saw online.
Rudolph: You need to keep an open mind.
Why?
Rudolph: Just follow me and admire LA.

Excuse me, but how can we possibly be in LA? I trust you, but this...
This is different. It doesn't look like what I saw on the internet.
Nice try. You seriously expect me to think this is real?
Did you spike my drink last night?
You did it to bring me here.
Rudolph: Here Kabar. Come on, heel! Show her what a good boy you are.
You've even found a dog that looks like him... with the same name.
Why are you shaking your head?
I don't believe it. This is ridiculous. I can't even say it.
Rudolph: Go ahead and say it.
It really is Kabar! Oh my God, Kabar and LA. So we're really in the twenties?
Rudolph: More precisely, June 30 1926. I've just finished with The Son of the Sheik.
Hey, wake up! You've fainted.
Where am I?
Oh God, what's going on? June 1926?
Are you dead or alive?
Rudolph: Alive.
She's fainted again.
She's not responding this time. Would you believe it! She finds my being alive more shocking than being in 1926. Who would have thought it? It's always been a bind understanding women, even from another time. Maybe that's what I love about them.
Ah, she's waking up.
You're alive. This is 1926. Don't say anymore, or I'll lose my senses again.
Rudolph: Come inside. Have a look round while you recover.
Is there any point in recording this? Won't the batteries run low?
Rudolph: Take this. You'll need it to keep recording.
I don't believe it. It was invented during your days! Something's not right here. No, don't say anymore.

Alright, give it to me. Now I'll describe everything. This gadget's so small. How do you turn it on?

Rudolph: It already is.

Transcribe everything on paper. Stop talking and just do it!

Okay.

Testing, testing!

Start narrative: Rudolph Valentino's house.

Stop laughing or I'll lose my concentration. I'm serious. A bit disorientated, but serious.

We're in the lounge. We ascended the stairs leading to the house, then went to the top floor. There are two other rooms, but this is the biggest.

The room is enormous. To our left are some huge stained glass windows. It all looks so Spanish.

I can't go on, this is all so distracting. I don't understand. How is this even possible? My hands are shaking. I'm scared!

Rudolph: Of what? You're with me now. Isn't that enough?

You wanted to be with me. You said that I neglected you. Now you're here, and here you'll stay.

But you said you were a ghost with a tormented past.

Rudolph: I know. You're going to get angry with me now. I lied! I couldn't take you to my home in 1926.

Yeah, and making me think I was talking to a ghost is perfectly normal!

Rudolph: Not normal, just unusual.

You've gone crazy, and I with you.

Maybe you're right. I should check out your house and distract myself. I'll get on with the description. There's a splendid suit of medieval armor at the door of the room. It's perfectly accurate. It couldn't be any other way, considering the owner's such a perfectionist.

There are two sofas standing back to back and facing opposite directions. You could sit and start small talk anywhere here. There's a huge portrait near the windows.

Who is it?

Rudolph: The duchess of the House of Savoy.

She was really beautiful.

On the opposite side, I can see an elegant grand piano. There's a nice Spanish shawl on top of it.

Where do these double doors lead to?

Rudolph: To a library. There's a dining hall just opposite it.

Of course. And after dining you come here for coffee.

Rudolph: Not really. This isn't Italy. Here, take a digestif or some liquor after eating. This is between us of course, as it's illegal and carries a prison sentence.

I hadn't thought of that. Of course, we're in the Prohibition years!

It all looks so European here.

Let's move on to the library.

There are two paintings here. The first shows Rudolph wearing the uniform of a Persian militiaman. The second shows him dressed up like an Argentinian gaucho.

Rudolph: Let me add that they were painted by a Cuban friend of mine, Federico Beltran-Masses.

Who? Sorry, I don't know him. Did he do Arte Deco?

Rudolph: Right. He was a famous painter who studied alongside Joaquin Sorolla at the École des Beaux-Arts de Barcelone. He painted landscapes, but became a superstar thanks to his paintings of celebrities. One of them is right before you!

He called the first painting you mentioned "The Black Falcon". I don't have the one showing me with Pola.

I almost forgot, there's a canvas on my bed depicting a famous Spanish ballerina. He did that too. I even got to know Irene, his beautiful wife. She paints too. She's from a well-to-do family. She really helped Federico with his career.

These paintings are amazing. He's got talent! Can I meet him?

Rudolph: He lives in France, Paris I think. We could go, but you need to remember that transport's a little slow here, and we'll need to go by boat.

You're right, I forgot. But if we go to Paris, we could visit Milan too.

I wonder what Milan's like these days. I think I'd barely recognize it.

There's just one problem. I might encounter my grandfather. Did you know he sang at the Scala Theatre? I can't remember what, but I think he had a part where he rode in on stage on a pony while playing a trumpet.

I need to think about whether it's worth it.

You mentioned Pola Negri. Are you still seeing her?

Rudolph: Jealous?

Yes, now that all your friends are still alive.

Rudolph: Very jealous, I see. I'll limit myself to saying I like that.

Tell me the truth! Are you intimate with her?

Don't play sly with me.

Even in 1926 I can get ticked off.

Why so quiet?

Don't go. What am I supposed to do here?

Oh no, I'm having a panic attack. I can't breathe!

I don't feel well.

Rudolph: What's happening?

Wait, I'll get some water.

Take this vitamin pill.

No!

Rudolph: Shut up and do as you're told!

Drink it all!

I don't have your antibodies.

Rudolph: I said drink.

Wait, your breathing's normal. You arched your eyebrow the way I do in The Four Horsemen of the Apocalypse *to indicate I'm lying. You had me there!*

Don't bother running, I'll catch you.

That door leads to the hall. You don't know what's behind the others! Oh, the bathroom. Not exactly romantic.

This sink is superb. You even have hot water. Can I try it?

Rudolph: Very funny. We're not cavemen you know. We have everything. I'll take you to the kitchen later and show you the walk-in refrigerator and cooker.

Do your bad guy face from The Son of the Sheik!

All right.

"I hate you!"

Rudolph: You keep this up and you'll end up in the bathtub.
Now let's fill it and change game.
I'm in Rudolph Valentino's bathtub. The furnishing's as classy as the rest of the house is. I can see the trees from the window. The curtains are made of silk, no doubt Italian. There's a stupendous dressing table where you can make yourself up with all kinds of perfume. The stool under it has some funny looking legs that look like elephant feet. The whole bathroom's mostly blue. I can see some clothes discarded on the floor. My eyes meet those of Rudolph. He's in the tub, his arms resting on the edges. His gaze is penetrating, leaving no escape for his prey. It's as if he can strip you down with a glance.
I can't stop gazing at him. I barely notice my clothes falling upon his.
Our lips search desperately for each other as my hand strokes him. My heart's racing. A feeling of impotence pervades every inch of me.
I could watch him for hours.
He's the most handsome, intriguing, sensual man I've ever...
Rudolph: Put that "gadget" down. The most sensual man in the world wants to show you that he's not forgotten why he's done this for you. Get in the tub. I had it installed three days ago because I knew you would come. Now let's see if I chose it wisely. The previous one was too small for two.
Oh you!

June 30 1926, 10:00 am

Hello world! I've just made love to Rudolph Valentino in 1926.
Look at you! I could kiss you all over. I'm the happiest person in the world.
Who said that dreaming's the only joy in life? This could only get better if we went for a drive in the Isotta.
How can I not be thankful for all this? Come here, I want to smother you with kisses.
I'm so happy!
If this is a dream, don't pinch me. I want it to last forever.

I now know what it means to let myself go, and that's all thanks to you. Nothing can hold me back now.

Rudolph: I don't think that's the only thing I taught you.

Don't say it. The microphone's on.

Rudolph: So what?

Remember that someone's going to read this.

Rudolph: Do you trust me?

Yes.

Rudolph: Then don't stop.

Shall we go to the bedroom?

Sure. Pass me the towel.

Rudolph: Put my robe on.

It suits you.

You looked better in it in the photos.

Will you put it on instead? For me?

Rudolph: I'll put on whatever you want.

This feels so unreal.

I still can't fully believe it.

I love you to death.

Let's go.

The bedrooms are downstairs, right?

Rudolph: Indeed. You've managed to get a feel for the place.

Your eyebrow's still raised.

Run, you 1920s buffoon.

You don't have the stamina.

Put me down! We could fall down the stairs.

Put me down you swine!

Rudolph: Where are you going? That's the guest's room!

Have you slept with another women in it?

Rudolph: No.

Then there's no problem!

Rudolph: Alright, let's go.

Was it worth the wait? You're starting to pick up my bad habits.

C'mon, answer me!

I'm not sure.

Rudolph: On the bed, you.

He's asleep.

I'm starving.

I'll head to the kitchen and grab something from the refrigerator he talked about.

He's a gift of nature. I've already mentioned his perfect physique, but I've never spoken about his beauty when sleeping.

He manages to give me multiple orgasm's throughout our intimacy.

Pure ecstasy.

If I were to die now, I'd die happy, knowing that I've experienced the strongest emotions possible.

Let's have a look at this house.

I'll definitely need to take the stairs. If the dining room is up there, then so will the kitchen.

There are so many weapons hanging on the walls. The bedroom had a rug, but everywhere else it's marble. The suits of armor lead towards the lounge, so I must be on the right track. There it is, a long wooden table filling the room. It's not so big, and it's surrounded by only four chairs. A great medieval style chandelier illuminates the room, and there's a beautifully carved oak sideboard against the wall. The little sailing ship model placed on it is charming. It looks like a caravel.

It's not exactly opulent, but it's certainly classy.

There it is!

Finally, the kitchen.

I'm surprised at how similar it is to our modern ones.

There's the cooker he spoke about. There are even two ovens.

The refrigerator dominates the room. It's huge!

Let's have a look inside.

So, he does eat meat after all. Look at how much there is! There's milk, eggs, cheese and fruit. I'll take some of that and give it a wash. I'll steer clear of the cheese. I imagine hygiene isn't too thorough in these days. I could be wrong though.

This apple will do nicely. Ooh, apricots too.

Paper napkins? Of course, there aren't any. Here they use cloth ones. A clean dish cloth's all I need. Now I'll head back to the bedroom.

Hey, I must have taken a wrong turn. I'm in the library!

Wow, look at all these books. How could I have missed this?

They look like collectors' editions.

There are some in French and German. I feel somewhat ignorant. I guess I must add "cultured" to his list of good qualities.

Now that I think about it, I can save myself the trouble of tracking down his books. They're all here!

His performances when playing sad characters were so convincing precisely because he didn't have them anymore.

I guess that's why he didn't want a mausoleum.

I still don't understand how this is all possible.

How can I be here? It's as if my present is now in the future.

I want to go home. What am I doing here?

What happens if I get sick?

Maybe he's right. I should distract myself, check out more of the house. He'll give me the answers I want in good time. I need to keep my mind busy. What day is this anyway? It's June in 1926 if I remember correctly. He dies on August 23. What will I do then, alone in this time?

I couldn't bear to see him die. It would be too much.

That's enough! I'll go and demand answers.

No need to rush. He's not exactly far.

I'm at the bedroom door and I have no idea what to do.

I'm afraid of what he might say.

Perhaps I could just shut out these thoughts and live idyllically in these days which will live on in my memories.

That's it! All this is so wonderful, so why spoil it?

I must forget everything, cancel out all fear. I'll try and find his own bedroom, but first I want to watch him a little.

He's still asleep. I don't want to miss a single opportunity to be with him.

I'll leave him in peace.

I wonder where his bedroom is.

There it is. The style's completely different. Very minimalist.

There's the painting of the Spanish ballerina.

She's beautiful in that seductive pose. Her arms are raised, her hands clasping above her head. They draw attention to her bare torso. Her body is stunningly graceful. Only a diaphanous veil covers her more intimate parts. Everything else doesn't leave anything to the imagination.

There's a chandelier in the middle of the room, but it's not the only source of light. There are some lamps on the furniture and one on the wall for emergencies. There's even a bracket lamp shaped like a candle. The drapes conceal both the windows flanking the bed and the French window by the entrance. There are two daybeds at the room's entrance, much too large for a smaller room. This room doesn't have the same vibe as the others. Perhaps it's the influence of his ex-wife Natasha Rambova.

I like the orange bedsheet. I think I'll stand on the bed and pose like the ballerina on the painting.

I place my robe on the bedside table and notice how soft the silken bedsheet is.

There's the tie. I'll need it to cover myself. I just have to lean on the pillows and raise my arms. Oh, I forgot. I need to face the door.

Rudolph: Not bad!

Oh, excuse me. I didn't want to come in here. Well, I did, but I thought I could get away with it.

Anyway, you're quite hot yourself.

Rudolph: What does that even mean?

That your incredibly handsome and cause a few heads to turn in your direction.

Rudolph: Interesting.

I half expected to wake up and have you bombard me with questions.

Instead, here you are relaxing on my bed. How does that even work?

What time is it?

Rudolph: Eleven thirty.

Let's have a bath and eat out.

I'm hungry!

Rudolph: Alright, let's talk about something else. Heck, let's get washed.

But isn't there anyone else in here?

Rudolph: I dismissed everyone for today.

June 30 1926, 12:00 am

We've had our bath, and now we're ready to go out.

We're passing through the courtyard, where we can hear the splashing of the fountain.

As I implied earlier, it's still there in 2015. Too bad for the house.

He's opening the gate. My heart's racing, my eyes are watering.

I know it's a strange reaction to have upon seeing a car, but I feel like I've hit the jackpot.

I can't take it. Those meters separating us feel like miles.

There it is!

Rudolph: Holy cow, I knew you liked it, but I didn't expect you to faint.

Wake up! I'm hungry too, you know.

C'mon, it's only a car. Ah, feeling better?

Get a grip. Everyone can see you. It's not exactly polite to hug the hood.

Please, let me worship it like the mechanical divinity it is. You've no idea what I'd have done in my days just to sit inside it. Yet here I am, just one step away from entering it. I'm over the moon.

Rudolph: So I see!

Glad to be of service. Get in.

First I want to get a good look at it from the outside.

Rudolph: You're not listening to me.

I'll never understand why the driver should get wet when it rains while the passengers can stay dry in the back seats.

Rudolph: You're wrong. The roof can be added to the front.

I didn't know that.

Do you remember that 1929 model? That was loaded with accessories. How's yours in comparison?

Rudolph: The interior's a little more threadbare, but it has a charm of its own. It's all sturdy, what with the leather seats. It even has curtains.
I know. I remember seeing them in that 1925 movie. You stripped down in it and lowered the curtains while putting on your swimsuit.
Rudolph: I'm a real seducer whilst doing it, don't you think?
Maybe. I didn't notice!
Rudolph: You raised your eyebrow again, so you're telling another whopper.
Quit the laughing.
I'm getting in!
I'm afraid of dirtying it.
I'm sat in the Isotta Fraschini. It seems so unreal.
What more could I want? I'm sat in the Isotta of my movie idol.
Rudolph: Can I get in too?
Of course, it's yours!
Rudolph: Why do you keep stroking it?
I'm starting to get jealous. You never paid this much attention to me.
Are you crazy? What are you doing putting your feet up on the bodywork?
Just admiring the roof.
Crazy indeed! Here I am with you in 1926, barely working out how it's possible.
I think that once the excitement passes, I'll get a panic attack.
Let's get moving before I start overthinking things.
Rudolph: Don't you want to know how it works?
Not now.
Will you buy me a silver pendant to hang the microphone on? It looks like a dongle.
Not that kind!
Stop laughing.
Let's go.
I'm hungry!
Rudolph: I'll take you to a place called "Musso & Frank's grill".
Alright.

Here we go.

This car's got a powerful engine. I felt its rumble. It has eight cylinders, and I've been able to admire them in all their beauty. It's music to my ears. As I let the sound transport me, we pass the stables through "Bella Drive".

Mary Pickford, his first American girlfriend, is one of his neighbors, as are Douglas Fairbanks and Buster Keaton. I can't remember where I read that!

We're now on Benedict Canyon Road. We're driving through some steep hills.

What's going on?

Rudolph: Slight problem, but I've got the tools to fix it.

I know you can handle it. I saw the photos.

Well, at least the view here's fabulous. The landscape's breathtaking.

Rudolph: It was nothing. We can set off again at any time.

Can I climb in?

Rudolph: Sure.

The driver's seat's on the right.

I only just noticed, although the journey wasn't that long.

Can I open the window?

Rudolph: Go ahead.

The winch's quite tough.

The car my father had when I was little also had winches to open the back windows.

Those were other times... even though they're technically in the future now.

Let's move on.

We're heading left now. I guess were going to Sunset Boulevard.

Rudolph: Correct!

Thank you.

There isn't much traffic here, is there?

Rudolph: Just wait and see!

We're turning.

Where are we now?

Rudolph: Hollywood Boulevard. We're almost there.

You were right. This is pure chaos. It's like driving through Cairo.

Rudolph: What's that city like?
It's beautiful, very beautiful. The pyramids are visible from the road. It seems impossible just by looking at them that man could have built something so ingenious. The traffic of course spoils the atmosphere with its lack of regulation.
I honestly get the same feeling here.
Rudolph: We do have regulations here you know!
Sorry, but it doesn't look like they're universally accepted.
Rudolph: Whatever.
Here we are. I'll park on some side road and we'll do the rest on foot. Remember, lower your head and get in quickly.
Okay.
My feet have finally touched the ground of Hollywood Boulevard.
Where now?
Rudolph: Back here.
Smells nice. I like this place.
The architecture of your time is fascinating. That of the previous decade isn't so bad either.
I feel overwhelmed by emotion.
Pinch me, I can't believe I'm here with you.
I feel like shouting to the world how much I love you.
Rudolph: Just remember what year this is.
Of course!
Can we hold hands?
Rudolph: Best not. We'd draw too much attention, and believe me, that's to be avoided.
Okay, let's go.
What's that guy doing? He's taking that woman's purse!
Rudolph: What do you think you're doing? You've knocked him out cold!
How do you say "Here's your purse" in English?
Rudolph: Just give it to her and take my hand.
Run!
What are you doing? Where are we running to?
Rudolph: I know a passageway. We need to get onto this house's roof. C'mon, start climbing.

You're going too fast. Why are we running?

Rudolph: I've been recognized.

You're right. They're calling for "Rudy".

Rudolph: Block the door. It won't hold for long, but we must jump to Musso's roof there.

You're crazy!

Rudolph: You've just hopped eighty-nine years into the past, and you're fretting over this lousy jump.

I just want to avoid ending up looking like a pancake.

Rudolph: What a wimp.

I knew appealing to your pride would work.

Stop it, you're hurting me. Stop hitting me, someone might see.

Why are you looking at me like that?

Rudolph: I'm getting the impression that sometimes you put on an act to make me feel more heroic. You don't really need to cling to me, do you?

Hah! You arched your eyebrow. I'm right!

You've really got to stop making that noise from The Four Horsemen of the Apocalypse.

Hands off, they're watching us! Don't touch my butt.

Rudolph: I didn't touch it, I slapped it.

Ooh, that's a fierce look.

Will you take my hand?

So I can now?

Rudolph: Sure, let's go the back way, then we can do as we please.

Are they Italian?

Rudolph: Yep, they opened a few years ago, I think in 1919.

Is this the kitchen?

Rudolph: Sure is.

Hi Frank.

Frank: Hi Rudolph.

Rudolph: Let me present the love of my life.

Frank: Is she the one you've been yakking on about this past year?

Rudolph: The same.

Anna, meet Frank.

Pleased to meet you.

Frank: The pleasure's all mine. It's an honor to meet you. Rudolph says you're special.

Thank you. I'm not used to all these compliments.

Ouch!

Frank: Your table's always free when I hear you're in LA.

Please, walk this way.

Do you already have an idea of what you want to order?

No, I need to ask Rudolph.

Frank: Alright. Here are the menus.

Thank you.

Why did you step on my foot?

Rudolph: This is 1926. Complimenting a woman is compulsory.

Knowing him, he'll probably want a private word with me to tell me what he thinks of you.

What if he says I'm not that good-looking?

Rudolph: Then he's blind!

Try touching my hand next time.

Rudolph: Sure. Sorry.

But when you start talking, the words pour out like a deluge.

Well, maybe you need to show me more of the ropes.

I'm hungry!

What can I eat without getting sick?

Rudolph: Anything you want.

Don't worry. It's one of the cleanest restaurants I know. The food's always fresh. They have huge refrigerators.

I saw them back in the kitchen.

I don't think my body can handle this water.

Rudolph: First off, it's in a glass bottle. Secondly, it comes from a nearby stream. Third, this isn't the goddamn Stone Age.

Just think that they spent 23,000,000 dollars just to set up the piping here.

Sure, keep laughing. You almost don't deserve any lunch.

Touchy.

Alright, I'm convinced.

Rudolph: Let's change subject. I find your attitude to our relationship annoying.

The chicken here's delish!
Oh, I forgot you don't eat meat.
I eat fish though.
Rudolph: Take the grilled salmon then. It comes with a nice sauce.
Even Charlie eats it.
Who?
Rudolph: Charlie Chaplin. Didn't I tell you we're friends?
You did.
That's so cool! I'd love to meet him and the others.
Rudolph: Sure, let's hold a party at my place. I'll introduce you to them.
Would you mind if I invited some women too?
Only the married ones.
No singles please.
Rudolph: There you go again.
Don't do that with your foot. Not here.
I can't control myself.
I can feel that. I think you'll have a hard time getting up now.
Rudolph: Stop it, or no lunch.
Alright, I'll stop.
Rudolph: Frank, a grilled salmon for two. Make it special.
Frank: For you, always!
I half expected him to kiss my hand.
Rudolph: He wouldn't dare in front of me.
That's true. I've seen your movies. The actress's husbands were jealous.
But it's not written in stone that his lips have to touch my hand when he does it.
Rudolph: You've seen my admirers. Do you really think I'd be so popular if I had limited myself to that?
I guess not! You weren't too subtle in expressing your passion.
Rudolph: You're so Mediterranean.
Where are you going?
I'll show you how Mediterranean I can be.
Rudolph: Sit down.

You need to get a grip of yourself. The last time I told you to keep calm you hauled off and punched a guy.
But... he was stealing a purse!
Rudolph: Some man would have dealt with it.
I hadn't thought of that.
Rudolph: What was that, anyway?
What?
Rudolph: What you did.
Oh, Karate.
Rudolph: Holy smokes, I've got to remember to never make you angry.
You're not lacking in strength or agility. I'll teach you a thing or two.
Tango versus Karate.
Rudolph: Obviously.
Poor kid. I imagine he'll never mug people again. I guess he realized that if women can punch like that, he'd better steer clear of men!
Your laugh is contagious. I've never had so much fun in my life.
How could I not be in love with you?
I could write poems about it.
Don't. They're our private feelings, and you should certainly not write them in your diary.
Rudolph: What? I don't have one. Do I look like the kind of guy who'd keep one?
Not really. You were never much of a writer.
Here comes the fish.
I could eat a horse.
He's got up. Frank's called him, just as he said he would. This restaurant's classy.
It's very elegant for a place specializing in grilled food.
The staff's so polite.
Will it still be around in 2015?
Who cares, I'm in 1926! Still, it would be nice if it still exists.
The food's superb.
The furniture's priceless.
It's clean, just as Rudolph said.

I can't even smell anything from the kitchen.
No health inspector's bringing this place down!
I brush my hand on the armrest. What a feeling.
The outer surface is made of wood, while the inner's covered in some soft fabric. The tablecloth's silk or some other similar material.
Nothing's fake.
Now that I think about it, I could go and get a nice nightgown made of silk, with natural colors. I could buy one in 2015, but it would be too expensive.
It's perfect. Now, should I use the present tense for 2015, or refer to it in the past, despite it being in the future? Oh well...
I wonder if I'll even be able to keep the nightgown on.
The restaurant has teardrop-shaped lamps, and the lighting's romantic.
I'm squinting to get a better look. It looks like a form of paneling covering the whole ceiling. Oh, that's exactly what is!
I get up to touch it. I know I shouldn't, but I can't help myself.
It's hand-carved. I can tell by the marks on it. The manager certainly didn't spare any expenses.
Even the beams on the ceiling are fantastic. There aren't many, but they're inserted so harmoniously, adding to the atmosphere.
I love it.
Hey, welcome back!
Rudolph: I'll tell you about it later.
Tonight I'm taking you to a place I know you'll really love. First we'll need to get some decent clothes, including underwear, a hat and some shoes.
What's wrong with the shoes I'm wearing now?
Rudolph: They're open. Not exactly in vogue these days.
You could just say I got them in Paris.
Rudolph: Don't you think it would be better to not draw attention to yourself?
Yes, of course, you're right.
Shopping in 1926!
I don't believe it.

But please don't spend too much.

Rudolph: What are you talking about? Believe me, money's the last thing on my mind.

Sorry, I didn't mean to offend you. It just came out.

Rudolph: Frank's gone to check if we can leave by the back door. We'll head to a store selling Coco Chanel products.

Let me drive. You can give me the directions in the back seat, with the curtains drawn.

Rudolph: You might find that difficult. Today's cars are difficult to maneuver. You really need to push down hard on the breaks and the gears are different.

You could teach me.

Wait!

Are you afraid that I'll ruin your Isotta?

Let me guess, women are dangerous in the driver's seat.

Rudolph: I'll explain on the way.

You know Rudolph, those vitamins you gave me are really something.

I think my skin's got more color now.

Rudolph: Glad to be of service.

Here we are.

Right, starting the engine.

Rudolph: Wait, hit the pedal.

Can I open the windscreen? It's not boiling, but it must be like seventy-eight degrees outside.

Rudolph: Go ahead. Let me help you.

Now, push down the pedal and get into gear.

Take the handbrake off!

Push down before accelerating. Just tap it.

We keep bumping.

No offence, but you can't handle LA's traffic, especially in a car you barely know. It's a long journey to our destination anyway.

Alright, you take the wheel.

Can I stay in the front with you?

Rudolph: It's a little unusual, but I like the idea.

I was concentrating so hard that I didn't get what you said.

You mentioned Coco Chanel.

Rudolph: I did.
I can barely contain my excitement.
Do you even know what that means to me?
Rudolph: I guess so.
We'll even buy the underwear I like.
You just want to kill me with excitement!
Can I sleep on your shoulder?
Rudolph: Sure. I'll wake you when we arrive. I just hope no one stares at us.
She's asleep.
These are without a doubt the strongest emotions she's ever felt. No wonder she's dozed off.
Oh, how I love her. I don't want her to know how deep my feelings for her go. Even I can't explain them.
I can't wait to start spending the rest of my life with her.
Every difficulty we'll face will become a challenge to be faced, a new way of seeing things.
I'm already savoring our every moment together.
I heard that.
Rudolph: You minx, I thought you were sleeping.
I wasn't.
Rudolph: Never mind. Now you know how I feel.
You've no idea how happy that makes me. It fulfils my every hope after seeing all the trouble you went through to get to me, and what you told your friends.
Rudolph: That's right.
Give me a kiss.
While driving?
Rudolph: Okay, later.
Are we there yet?
Rudolph: Almost. The car's these days aren't as fast as yours.
It doesn't matter. They're wonderful.
I've been thinking. I don't want any of those conservative-looking clothes women wear here.
Rudolph: No swimsuit then.
Alright, get me the least conservative then.
And the underwear, of course.

Rudolph: Leave that to me. I'm an expert.
What's with that face? Jealous? You know what I'm like. I'd be lying if I told you I'm a saint.
I know. Just don't remind me.
Rudolph: Let's just say you'll wear the one I say suits you.
Alright.
Rudolph: I've already decided what dress you'll have.
Okay. I'm going to sleep now, and this time I mean it.
Rudolph: Sweet dreams.
Thanks.
Rudolph: Rise and shine. We've arrived.
Oh no, you're impersonating me from last year's movie, the scene where I wake up and realize it's late.
You won't get away with this. Let's go.
What's up?
I'm frightened. I've seen plenty of people today, but she...
I can't stop thinking about the fact that she's dead.
Rudolph: Well, she's alive now, and you've not even been born yet.
Okay, when you put it like that...
Rudolph: It's not how I put it, it's just the way it is!
Shop assistant: Hey, aren't you Rudolph Valentino?
Rudolph: The very same. Could you show us some dresses for the lady here? Preferably in a private room.
Shop assistant: Certainly. This way please.
Make yourselves comfortable. I'll send in Madame Florant.
I almost had a panic attack, Rudolph. Do you have this effect with everyone?
Rudolph: I guess so. You should know by now.
Shut up! Oh, sorry. I didn't mean it.
Rudolph: Don't worry, just keep your cool, especially when others are around.
Yes, sorry again.
Rudolph: Madame Florant.
I've come here because it's said you have the latest in Parisian fashion.

We'd like a Coco Chanel if you don't mind, and I wish to accompany the lady to the changing room, as her English is a little rusty... if you don't mind of course.
Madame Florant: As you wish.
Rudolph: I'd like her to try the dress I saw back there, the one which exposes the back.
Madame Florant: Excellent choice. It's not something all women can wear. You have impeccable taste. Here it is.
Rudolph: Take it. Put it on, for me.
Do I need to do anything in particular?
Rudolph: Just don't let the excitement get to you.
Alright.
Rudolph: How long do you need?
I'm almost ready. I had a hard time figuring out how to put it on.
Rudolph: Wow! What a stud.
What? You don't use that word for women.
Rudolph: Stop laughing.
Okay, I messed up. Nothing worse than the stuff you come out with. You've ruined the atmosphere.
Still, you look pretty sexy, like Louise Brooks. She made her debut last year. Quite talented.
I know her. I hope for your sake she's just an acquaintance.
Rudolph: Naturally.
You're enchanting when you put in the effort.
It's all about body language.
Rudolph: You know there could be people listening, right?
Keep speaking in Italian then.
Come here, I need to whisper something to you.
I feel like a stud.
Rudolph: You're a blast. There's no way I'm going to die this year.
I won't let you.
The dress is green, my favorite color. There's an opening at the back which leaves the back exposed. Still, it hugs me sensually and brings out my figure. The front is smooth, except for the collar, which forms a kind of shawl. The arms are free to show off their slenderness.

All that's missing is a hat.
Rudolph: Rather than the usual cloche hat, why not take this one with feathers on top?
I'm not sure.
Rudolph: C'mon, try it.
You look like a diva.
You go too far. Thank you for your kind words, but I don't see it that way.
Rudolph: Alright, I'll keep my mouth shut.
I'd appreciate that.
Rudolph: When the party's over, I'd take great pleasure in undressing you.
Now let's look over the lingerie.
Madame?
Madame Florant: Magnificent, a superb choice Mister Valentino. Anything else?
Rudolph: Yes, some lingerie.
Madame Florant: Still from Paris?
Rudolph: Yes. Get us the most sensual you have.
Do you have any corsets? Like the ones that were in vogue a few years back?
Madame Florant: I'll check. The sizes might be a touch too large, as they're more popular with aged ladies. Do you require a particular color?
Rudolph: Definitely red, with some black and white on it.
Madame Florant: A moment please.
Rudolph: Get changed. Soon you'll be trying on the underwear.
Alright.
Madame Florant: I've brought some panties to match. I've found this silk lace corset. The suspenders are particularly elaborate. They're held up by whalebones.
This model comes with either buttons or laces. I brought you both versions.
The button version comes in the color you asked for.
I'll take them to the lady and leave you.
Rudolph: You're too kind.
I can't get this waspie on.

Rudolph: It's called a corset. I'm afraid the waspie is yet to be invented.
Alright, this "corset" then.
Rudolph: Let's just say that the red one with laces is "inviting".
Why aren't you wearing the panties?
I refuse. They're huge. I need to whisper something else to you. It's not polite, but it needs to be said.
Try to hold back. I can see what you're thinking. The next time we go shopping, don't wear such tight trousers.
Rudolph: Understood. Try the panties. We need to buy them. You won't have to wear them if you really don't like them.
Alright.
Rudolph: They are of course different from what you're used to.
I once read that only the women working on the streets wore them.
Rudolph: Don't wear them then.
Of course.
Rudolph: You know what the best thing about these times is?
What?
Rudolph: There are plenty of hiding places.
I like what you're getting at. So, what are we waiting for?
Rudolph: Try the lingerie on. I'll find a way to keep my mind occupied.
We'll take everything.
Madame Florant: Would you care to see some more exclusive merchandise?
Rudolph: Yes, purses and gloves which match well with the dress. Add a transparent dressing gown, the kind popular with the flappers.
Madame Florant: Certainly.
Rudolph: That dressing gown's a hoot!
Excuse me Madame, I didn't mean to offend.
Your clothes are ideal for any situation, and I'll certainly recommend them to all my acquaintances.
Madame Florant: Once the lady's ready, we'll offer her a cup of tea she can enjoy while we wrap everything up.
Rudolph: As you please.

Follow the assistant.
I don't want to.
Rudolph: That wasn't a request. I need to put all of this on my tab.
Sorry, I misunderstood. I'm really ignorant of your ways.

June 30 1926, 4:30 pm

The car's stuffed with packages of all sizes. There's even a pink hatbox in the back seat. The trunk's completely packed. Shopping in 1926 isn't so different from what I'm used to. The only real difference is just how soft the fabrics are. Nobody can claim to have chosen such clothes more expertly than Rudolph has done.
The day's barely done, but we're both tired out. The return journey's a long one. Maybe we'll just chill tonight. It would be better to call everything off until tomorrow.

July 1 1926, 9:00 am

Rudolph: What's all this screaming?
Where is she?
She's left her microphone on the pillow.
Mariella the cook: Mister Valentino, forgive the disturbance, but please come quickly.
Rudolph: Right behind you!
Mariella: There's a woman in the bath. She's fainted and... naked.
Rudolph: No surprises there, but she's thrown up this time. Go get some water please. When she regains her senses I'll give her a "cachet".
Mariella: Right away.
Rudolph: Actually, I'll give her a tranquilizer. Looks like she still hasn't got over being in 1926.
Mariella: Is she an actress?
Rudolph: She isn't.
Mariella: But she's so beautiful.
Rudolph: I know. I'll make her my wife as soon as I can.

124

Mariella: Congratulations!
Rudolph: Thank you. I'll take her to my room now.
Mariella: Shall I prepare breakfast?
Rudolph: Yes please. Till later.
Wake up, my love.
Hi.
Rudolph: Good morning dear.
How're you feeling?
I can't say.
Rudolph: The next time you decide to get up, please have the common courtesy to tell me first. You shouldn't walk around in the nude.
You said you dismissed everyone!
Rudolph: Sure, yesterday. Obviously not today though.
I know, I saw a woman leave.
Rudolph: Take this pill.
More vitamins?
Rudolph: No, it'll just relax you.
Okay.
Rudolph, I miss my home.
I miss my entire family.
I miss everything.
They'll be worried sick about me!
How can I possibly keep calm about this?
Rudolph: Write about it in your book! Dedicate a message to your family, telling them that you're in 1926, that you're in perfect health, and that you miss them, as unbelievable as it all sounds.
How will they be able to read it?
Rudolph: Someone you know, like Fiorella, who remembers the title, will find it online or on a bench.
At least you remember what the internet is.
Alright, but how am I going to publish it? It's a little raunchy for this period!
Rudolph: We'll spread the word among the moonshiners that there's an "audacious" book written in Italian which you can get

under the counter. It'll be a hit, just like all forbidden things. Your day will come.

Of course, these are the prohibition years. Al Capone's still around.

Rudolph: Would you like to meet him?

Absolutely not.

Rudolph: He's currently facing trial in Chicago for murder, among other things. They'll never nail him.

Trust me, they'll get him for tax evasion.

I'll need to write a glossary of 21st century terminology. It won't be easy. No one these days knows what they mean.

I'll have to use a pseudonym, otherwise they'll trace it back to us.

Rudolph: No, use your real name. We'll assume different identities in any case.

After August 23, we'll move house and assume new names.

Thank God. So you're not going to die?

I wouldn't have stood for it.

Rudolph: Let's hope. It's all arranged.

They're sculpting a wax figure of me, which they'll show off during my funeral. We'll say it's staying there until my corpse has been prepared.

Clever!

Rudolph: I just hope your antibiotics work.

On that note, you'll have to carry them with you always, so you can hand me them when necessary.

Count on it.

Where are they?

Rudolph: In a little beauty case I took from your house.

I didn't know.

Did you bring some clothes too?

Rudolph: All but one. The rest's in the new house.

Where is it?

Rudolph: I can't tell you, or better, I'll whisper it to you, but you can't disclose it in the book.

I understand.

But I don't know anything about farming.

Rudolph: I'm the expert. I may have been a rake at school, but I loved farming.

Agriculture, right?

Rudolph: Yep. I went to the B. Marsano Agricultural College in San Ilario.

I even bought a tractor and a thresher, tons of stuff, all motorized. You'll see it'll be a walk in the park.

One day, you'll stop being surprised by everything, though I admit I'll miss that look you have when you see something new.

What year is this?

1926.

I see.

What will we call ourselves?

Rudolph: There's still time to decide what we'll put in our documentation. In any case, I've already chosen a name for myself.

Will you need to change your appearance?

Rudolph: Yes, I'll stop gelling my hair.

So they'll be scruffy then.

Rudolph: Very. I'll also need to have them cut.

Don't, I beg you.

Rudolph: It'll be necessary for a while, sorry.

Can I ask you something else?

Rudolph: Sure. Go ahead.

When will you explain everything to me?

Rudolph: After August 23. Can you wait?

It's hard, but I'll try.

Rudolph: C'mon, let's go to bed. We'll rest a little then have breakfast.

Good idea. I'm famished.

Rudolph: That's the spirit.

Are we staying in tonight, or are we going out?

Rudolph: Okay, after breakfast we'll do some sport.

Here as well? You're obsessed with it. Can't we do some under the bedsheets?

Rudolph: No. It doesn't matter what year this is, you need to keep in shape.

I hate you.

At least the exercise bike isn't here!
What's with that look? Don't tell me you've got one!
No offence, but you really stress me out. You've been like this the moment we first saw each other... or felt each other. I couldn't see you at first.
Alright, let's get this over with.

July 1 1926, 12:00 am

I'm shattered.
All that's sport's drained me.
You have real stamina.
Give me back my exercise bike, the only gym tool I actually like.
I'm hungry.
I feel like I haven't eaten in months. Okay, I'm exaggerating. Two days of fasting is enough to bring about the hunger I'm feeling now.
After eating I'm going to bed.
I can't handle your rhythm.
Rudolph: Are you sure you're asleep?
No, so what? I have rights you know! Including the one to vote.
Don't look at me like that!
Okay, we'll stay awake.
Or maybe not, I don't know.
Stop laughing, I'm thinking.
Let's go grab a bite to eat.
Stop it, or it'll get cold by the time we finish.
Rudolph: You know what I like about you?
What?
Rudolph: Your stubbornness.
Screw you.

July 1 1926 3:00 pm

Rudolph: C'mon dear, time to go.
Why?
Rudolph: Get your shoes.

128

Shall I drive?
Rudolph: Hands off my crown jewels.
Speaking of jewels...
No need. I have the microphone hanging on my neck. I have your mother's cameo too. It was kind of you to give it to me.
Rudolph: Want some flowers?
No. It's a shame to pick flowers.
Rudolph: Let's get changed and head off.
Tomorrow I'll show you the new house.
I'll miss Falcon Lair. It was the first thing I saw in 1926.
However, the main thing is being with you, regardless of location.
Rudolph: You still need to decide what name you'll assume.
I can't do that out of respect for my late sisters. It's not easy tracking people down in this period, so I'll keep both my name and surname. What will you call yourself anyway?
Rudolph: Raffaello... Just don't write it.
Not bad. So I'll be Mrs. Guglielmi.
Rudolph: You shouldn't have!
You really thought I wouldn't have figured it out by now?
Rudolph: Why are you giggling?
I thought that our names would look ridiculous on the intercom, but then I remembered it hasn't been invented yet.

July 1 1926 8:30 pm

I'm ready for my triumphal exit.
The green dress shows off my back and some part of my butt, and I'm wearing a pair of fantastic Mary Jane shoes to match. They're embroidered with precious stones, which even feature on the Cuban heel. My hair's bunched up with a fascinator sporting white feathers, which I wear sideways. The garment includes a jewel and pearl-encrusted purse and some fishnet gloves. I don't have the long necklace usually worn with such clothes.

Underneath I'm secretly only wearing suspenders which hold up a pair of marvelous silk stockings with a vertical line sewn on the back.

Nothing else.

I can the friends Rudolph invited to join us in our trip approaching.

I'm near the door leading to the garden.

I'm having some trouble with the dress, but I'll try to not look too awkward.

Now I'll approach him and wait to be introduced.

Good evening Rudolph. I'm ready to go.

Rudolph: Anna, meet Mary and Joseph.

Delighted. Rudolph has told me nothing but good things about you.

Mary, your dress is truly wonderful. If Rudolph would care to translate, I'd like to know where you got it from.

Hopefully, he'll limit himself to just saying that, won't you!

Rudolph: I'm stunned. You liar, I've never spoken to you about them. And what's got into you? You're talking like you've always lived here.

Yes Rudolph, let me have some fun. Could you please translate everything but the last part?

Rudolph: Be thankful I'm feeling generous, but just you wait. Once we arrive at our destination, you'll be the one left wide-eyed.

Okay, I've told her.

No, don't ask me, Joseph. She's no actress. I'll be marrying her as soon as possible.

They're congratulating us.

For what?

Rudolph: Our upcoming wedding.

What are you saying?

You weren't joking?

Your eyebrow's arched again. You're not kidding.

My dear, when the night's done, you'll suffer the same fate as the purse thief.

Rudolph: Let's go!

I'm calm. I need to get a grip of myself.

My God, I don't believe it. It's the Cotton Club.

Rudolph: Shut your mouth, or the flies will get in it.

I'm going to faint again. Hold me.

Rudolph: Here we are. Allow me to help you out of the car.

Charming.

Rudolph: That was... expressionless.

I'm getting in character.

It seems impossible.

I'm at the Cotton Club in 1926. It's not the New York branch, but maybe it's better, seeing as Rudolph goes there.

Charleston, Blues, pure fun! Sorry.

Rudolph: We'll need to get you an English tutor. You'll need to be able to speak for yourself. I can't interpret all the time. It's unbecoming of me.

Yes, you're right.

Make sure he isn't too old.

Rudolph: Who said it was going to be a "he"?

Jealous again?

Rudolph: Whatever.

I can't describe what's going through my head right now. I feel so alive, so happy, I could go crazy.

The place is so elegant, so classy. There are candles set in crystal orbs on every table. The tables are round and covered with blue silken tablecloths. They're organized in a horseshoe formation, giving space to anyone willing to dance or sing publicly.

What a show!

Rudolph: It hasn't even started yet.

It's a metaphor.

Rudolph: The place was called "The Green Mill" up until a few months ago. They built it in 1923.

There's even a private orchestra.

Oh, before I forget, if we end up staying the night, they'll offer us breakfast.

You can even drink something stronger if you grease the right palms here.
No way. I don't fancy being arrested. I'm a teetotaler anyway.
Rudolph: True. How boring. You don't drink, smoke, or eat meat. What do you enjoy anyway?
I'll show you when we get home.

July 1 1926, 11:50 pm

I'm shattered. Dancing the Charleston is more draining than alcohol. I don't dance it well, but I manage. The dress I'm wearing doesn't exactly help. I had to hold it up throughout the night. Now they're playing the tango. I'd love to learn it.
Rudolph: Tomorrow we'll have our first lesson then! In any case, isn't that how this all started? You wanting to dance with me?
Actually that came second place. We've done plenty of the first.
Rudolph: True.
Tomorrow, or today rather, after we're done resting, we'll go and see our new house. I'm certain you'll love it.
May I dance with Mary?
Only because I want to see you dance the tango. Won't it be a little like *The Four Horsemen of the Apocalypse*?
Rudolph: I suppose so.
I watched that movie selecting the correct frame speed. The online versions are speeded up.
It's amazing as it is watching him do the tango onscreen, but it's quite something else to see him do it in person.
He's a legend! I don't mean his movie presence, but his ability to infuse his every movement with sensuality. I've never seen anything so pleasurable. He'll have to go through some solo steps with me. Why is he so perfect? The man's an alien.
Obviously the world is full of men like him, but I've never met them. He's even a clean freak. He's coming. What now?
Rudolph: How was I?
How long before we can go home?
Rudolph: I'll take that as a "well". I sense a sudden interest in me.

132

Tas, as they'd say in Milan. Shut your hole.
Oh, they're doing the Charleston again. I need the distraction.

July 2 1926, 4:00 am

It's torture to my bones. My whole body aches and I can't wait to collapse in bed. Maybe torture's a little too strong a term, but it fits.
Rudolph: They're offering breakfast. Want some?
Sure, I could eat it all. These croissants are nice. I'd like two, plus a glass of milk with a little coffee. No offence, but the coffee here's different from ours.
Rudolph: No argument there.
I'm famished too. Let's take double of everything.
Even your friends are starving! Tell them it's been an absolute pleasure knowing that, and that next time we meet I'll be able to talk to them without help.
Thank you so much.
Shall we go?
Rudolph: Sure. I'm tired too. I'd like to avoid appearing on the front pages with bags under my eyes.
When though?
Rudolph: Maybe tomorrow.
We'll get a cab, but first let's say bye to Mary and Joseph.
Anna and I bid you good night. I hope we'll meet again soon. Give Mea Murray and David Mdivani my regards. I know you'll bump into each other one of these days.
I haven't seen them since their wedding two weeks ago. Goodnight again, and don't stay up too late. Kiss your daughter for me.
Mary: Certainly. Too bad we can't converse with Anna. Just tell her she has a beautiful smile. Goodnight to you both.
Rudolph: Come on you sluggish baby boomer, we'll lose our cab!
Are you mocking my wheezing?
No, you're arching your eyebrow again.
Rudolph: Stop, please. My fans want me whole! I have to attend the premiere of one of my movies.

133

Get in, or someone else will be taking this cab.

July 2 1926, 12:00 pm

Don't wake me. I'm in a coma.
Rudolph: C'mon, it's late, and lunch is served.
I don't care. Leave me in peace.
Rudolph: You know who's standing before you? Rudolph Valentino, naked. Does that energize you?
Ah, she's opened an eye. What's the big idea? Now they're both open. What the... get off, lunch is...!

July 2 1926, 1:00 pm

It'll be cold now. Shall we go?
Rudolph: This is the life! I want every day to be this intense.
Are you going to show me the now house as you said you would?
Will there ever be day in which we just chill out?
Rudolph: Yes to both.
Perfect! Now, I'm hungry.
The roaring twenties are doing wonders for my figure, though my belly's just a little big.

July 2 1926, 3:00 pm

We're heading off in the legendary Isotta Fraschini. We're passing through Santa Monica, though I can't disclose our destination. Rudolph says that someone might believe what I write, and that said person could turn up at our doorstep. The prospect of his mostly young female fans dropping by really gets to me. Still, for reasons unknown, it feels like my body's in reverse gear. I feel much younger. Maybe it's just a sensation or an effect of the clothes I now wear. Perhaps it's the vitamins. Never mind. I feel in shape.

134

The road's long and evening's upon us, but we're almost there. And now my "Cicero" has started narrating the rest of the journey in his inimitable way.

Rudolph: There it is! Majestic, don't you think?

It sure is!

Rudolph: It was designed in record time by a friend from the Wisconsin's Richland Center.

His name's Frank Lloyd. Heard of him?

Of course I have, he's a famous architect.

Rudolph: I knew this was the kind of house you liked, so I had him build it to your tastes. Truth be told, I wanted to install stained-glass windows, like those of Louis Sullivan, but he doesn't design them for home use, and there was no way I could change his mind. Just so you know, it's based on the Robie House in Chicago, built sometime around 1908 and 1910.

Can I describe it?

Rudolph: Be my guest!

The outside is stunning. It has multiple floors, and looks almost alive. The bricks are exposed on both the house and the walls surrounding it.

Other notable features are the balconies and windows, positioned in such a way that no landmark outside is invisible.

The garden's well tended and, as in Falcon Lair, the trees are Italian imports. Backbreaking work for a groundskeeper!

Behind the house I see a series of fields.

They appear to be each dedicated to the cultivation of different crops, though I don't know which kind. I'll have to ask.

Walking back to the house, I notice that there is no fence, just a main entrance. The door is made of hand-forged cast iron. The style reminds me of Liberty's, and can also be seen on the windows.

There's a rope attached to a bell for anyone wanting to announce their arrival. The chime sounds strange.

Have the servants ever told you that you look like Rudolph Valentino?

Rudolph: Sorry, but a scruffy beard and hair are necessary to hide my identity. And call me Raffaello in future.

Your third name!

Rudolph: Yes. As always, I ask you to keep a lid on your emotions. You'll like it here, and as we'll be living together the servants could find your displays a little shocking.

As you say!

Rudolph: Amelia, allow me to present my wife Anna.

Well, at least I make better first impressions now. At least she isn't a young girl.

Rudolph: I've thought of everything.

So I see.

Rudolph: Even the gardener's old.

I understand. The interior's really minimalist, just as I like it, while the furniture and the lamps are in the liberty style.

Amelia's a good cook.
Rudolph: Indeed. She takes from her mother, Denise. I didn't tell you this before, but she taught Amelia a little Italian, as well as our national dishes.
That explains a lot.
Rudolph: I hired Italians so that you wouldn't feel homesick. Come here. Let me hold you as we watch the stars. I wish this moment would never end.
I'm living the impossible, so as far as I'm concerned every wish can be granted. I love you.
Rudolph: That's Ursa Major there.
Is there anything you don't know?
Rudolph: Sorry, I wanted to present myself as an expert on everything, but it's impossible to lie to you.
I've always loved culture and cultured people. I like learning, so anyone with an education is in my mind one step ahead of everyone else.
Don't you find that minds can be just as sexy as bodies?
Rudolph: I should hope so, considering I'm not exactly on the tall side.
Anyway, there's no need to show off. I already have a high opinion of you.
Hug me tighter. I want to watch the stars in silence to better preserve this moment in my mind. My memory's not great, but I hope I'll never forget this.
I can hear crickets!
If this is a dream, don't wake me.
Rudolph: Let's get back inside. A breeze is coming. Shall we?
Help me up.
Can I take a closer look at the fields tomorrow?
Rudolph: Yes. Giovanni will show you around and explain everything.
Perfect. Let's go to bed now.
Rudolph: Right behind you.

Thank you for everything. The house is wonderful. It reflects my character. It's as if I myself furnished it! I have no idea how you got to know me so well, but I must say you've read my mind.
Is this the bedroom?
Rudolph: Yes. I had a daybed installed in it, even if the room's not that big. I put it there so I can watch you at a distance while you sleep.
Ten dollars a ticket.
Rudolph: Dammit, do you even know what you can get with ten dollars here?
Of course, I keep forgetting we're in the twenties. Let's say a dollar then. Still steep.
Rudolph: Done deal! I'll get ourselves a safe for banknotes.
Come here. I want to snuggle.
My head rests on his chest and I can hear his heart beating. His muscles are like hills my face can bury itself in. His skin is soft, and it sometimes tickles when his hairs touch me. My nose itches!
Stroking his chest is reassuring and comforting, like home, which is far ahead in the future.
But isn't home where the heart is?
This moment's all mine.
I think he feels the same way. I can sense an emotion of such depth in the air that you could almost touch it.
It's love, a great love, warm, towering and enveloping.
His lips caress my neck and I feel goosebumps on my skin. As they rise onto my shoulders, I feel the warmth of his breath charge my senses.
Quiet moans full of emotion come uncontrollably from my lips.
No part of my body is idle in this dance.
My physical expressions of my life are obvious to all.
Till later.

July 3 1926, 10:00 am

Rudolph: Now you'll go with Giovanni to the fields. Could you pass me the microphone please?

Why? You can't expect me to remember everything he tells me.
Rudolph: There's no need to add it to the book.
Alright.
There's the tractor you told me about!
Rudolph: Yes, and it's not the only tool we have.
Giovanni, could you give Anna a tour of the place? Tell her about the machines too. She's really into modern technology.
Giovanni: Yes sir. I'll even show her the granaries and our harvest.
Rudolph: Thanks, see you later.
Giovanni: Alright Mrs. Guglielmi, I'll tell you what we're...
Rudolph: I had to stay behind to leave this message.

Hello my love. I'm watching you as you walk through the fields. You're as curious as always. I don't know if I'll be coming back from New York, so I've decided to leave you with this.
These last few days have been the best of my life. I've never felt anything so intense. I feel like I could burst.
You've filled my life and made it bloom. Everywhere I go I'm overwhelmed by the scents and colors.
I wish this could last forever.
It's in moments like these that I ask myself what I've done to deserve such happiness.
Then I look at you and see my destiny.
I'll hold you close for all the time leading up to August 23rd, then I'll come back to you. As you yourself said, there's no other way about it. Wait for me, my love. I'll be back.
Hi Rudolph, erm, Raffaello. I've just found out that everyone knows I'm Mrs. Guglielmi. Why did you keep your surname?
Rudolph: I thought that if someone noticed the similarity, I could just say I'm one of Rudolph Valentino's relatives. Sorry if I'm only telling you now.
Clever.
Rudolph: We need to go to the bank today to give your signature. You'll be permitted to use my account. You'll be able to make any transaction you want until I return. Money is no issue

and don't worry about creditors. Everything here is paid for. You'll find all our receipts in the safe.

You're awfully serious.

Rudolph: So should you be this morning. Anyway, we'll be back in LA in three days, and we'll throw a party. Then we won't have a single worry in the world.

When can we go to the beach?

Rudolph: The day after the party, when they refurbish the house.

Let's organize a picnic. I haven't had one since I was a little girl. We used to go and have sandwiches at the water park in Milan, where there was an artificial lake. It was so fun. My aunts came, along with my cousin Annamaria.

My cousin's daughter Samantha is only nine, yet she does paragliding. Do you remember her?

Rudolph: Sure, you showed me the photos.

You're right, I keep forgetting things.

Alright, let's go. I can't say I'm eager, but at least I'll learn how banking transactions go here.

July 9 1926, 10:00 am

The days spent in this house have been unforgettable. Rudolph has told me what I'll need to do in New York. I'll get to know his assistant, who's been quite distant lately. I'll be spending a lot of time with him alone.

We're heading home now, as tonight there's the premiere of *The Son of the Sheik.*

Too bad I can't go. I'd have liked to take part.

Rudolph: Says who?

Didn't you say you preferred it if no one saw us together in public?

Rudolph: I've already got a seat reservation for you in an angle where I can keep an eye on you. You can't imagine how excited I am over you seeing me act here, now, in 1926.

Thank you so much for everything.

Rudolph: Please wear what you took to the Cotton Club.

With pleasure.

Rudolph: Once we get back, we'll have to hurry. I'm expected at two.
So no exercise today?
Rudolph: When we get back, yes. Don't wear anything underneath, just like last time, you hear? We weren't able to do anything last time because we were so exhausted, but this time I don't want to miss a second of you taking it off.
Yes boss.
Let's go.
When will we go horse riding?
Rudolph: Soon.
I'm back, Kabar! Oh, I'll miss you so much. C'mon my love, out in the garden with us.
I can't, you know I'm allergic.
Rudolph: Not anymore.
How do you know?
Rudolph: Just come out.
I don't know what's more grating; your aura of mystery or your constant machoism.
Hey, no fair! It's two against one.
Help! I've fallen and Kabar's licking me.
Rudolph: You served yourself on a silver platter.
Stop talking, or the microphone will record everything.
Rudolph: Too late.
Hey, get off me. We'll be late.
Rudolph: What is it you people from 2015 say?
Oh yeah, who gives a damn!

July 9 1926, 12:30 am

C'mon, we're late.
How do I look?
Rudolph: Perfectly fine.
Rudolph, did you just empty a whole perfume bottle on yourself?

Rudolph: Sorry, but today I need to play a part and, as you well know, the great Rudolph Valentino uses a lot of perfume.
What for?
Rudolph: I can't explain it. I just feel safer with it on.
You don't need it.
Rudolph: I know that now.
Let's go. The cab's waiting.
I never realized just who he was until now, despite his advances on me. Once we arrived at the entrance there were photographers everywhere. The women went crazy at the sight of him. Throughout the screening, they wouldn't stop hyperventilating. It's amazing to see his movies on the big screen. I'd previously seen him only on YouTube. I suppose they're right to get all emotional. He's the most handsome and provocative man I've ever known. He looks just like the adventurous Sheik he plays in the movie.
Oh God, I'm having trouble breathing too!
I didn't know someone would read the texts appearing on the screen during the projection. That was a big surprise for me.
The movie's finished, and I need to meet him at the end of the corridor, as I imagine everything will go bonkers once he appears.
Here he comes.
Rudolph: Thank you for the affection you always show for me. It's been an honor reciting with Vilma in this movie. She's been a marvelous colleague, just as she was when I worked on The Eagle.
I'd also like to thank everyone who accompanied us in this adventure.
My heart leaps when I think of all those women who believe in me. I blow a kiss to them all.
But most of all, I'd like to thank my muse, who inspired me throughout the movie's production. It is she who shares in my happiness now and with whom I couldn't live without. I love you Anna.
I managed to translate every word. It's clear he wanted me to understand.

I'm awe-struck. Any lingering doubts I had have been done away with. A murmur rises from the crowd. I luckily don't understand anything being said. I don't think I've ever felt so moved.
Rudolph Valentino loves me!
I must find a way to repay him.

July 9 1926, 10:00 pm

The hall's empty. What am I supposed to do?
Stranger: Anna Piccolini?
Yes.
Stranger: Mister Valentino is waiting.
I must find the courage to say something in English. I'll be alone for a few days after all.
Rudolph: Sorry dear, but I have to dine with the troupe to celebrate. This gentleman will accompany you home. I ask only one thing, and that's for you to stay dressed as you are when you go to bed.
Alright. I'll sleep fully clothed.

July 10 1926, 3:00 pm

The house is in chaos. We're preparing for tomorrow's party.
Although I think I will know the guests by name, I won't look them up. I quite fancy being surprised.
He'll present me as some relative from Italy.
We now have all our new documentation, so I was officially born on May 28 1895. It's so fun. I feel like I've been reborn. It's all a big game to me. I just home I don't end up missing what I left in 2015.
Everything's run smoothly so far. Every day brings new excitement and novelty. How could I get depressed in such a situation? It's impossible!
Rudolph: Come. We need to get two new dresses.
On Saturday evening?
Rudolph: Yes, we're expected. I phoned them and they'll keep the store open just for us. Being Rudolph Valentino has its perks!

143

Are we going to Madame Florant's again?

Rudolph: Yes. You'll just have to try them on. I gave her instructions for when you arrive, so I won't be there during the fitting. I want it to be a surprise for me too.

Rudolph, they're beautiful. Which one shall I wear tomorrow? Red or white?

Red.

Where now? What a strange place.

Rudolph: I think there's something missing on your finger.

What? Oh no, gold is too much. You've already spent enough on me. Thanks, but I can't accept.

Rudolph: Come with me in this office and I'll explain everything.

Looks like a cross between a chapel and a registry.

What is this place?

Why are you kneeling?

Rudolph: We're in a Marriage License Bureau. Will you marry me?

What kind of question is that? Of course I will.

Rudolph: Put on the white dress and bunch up your hair with this hairpin.

This dress hugs my figure, and is made entirely of lace. The neckline's round and doesn't show anything off. It's long and unfashionable for the times. Most dresses these days end just below the knees. I also have a coronet, like the one the Tsaritsa wore in the last decade. It's similar to the one worn by Vilma Banky in *The Eagle*.

I'm ready. I don't know what excites me more; what's going to happen or the desire for him to see me as I am now. I need to get a hold of myself.

It's not like marrying Rudolph Valentino is an everyday activity. No siree.

Oh, and I need to remember to call him Raffaello.

Rudolph: My God!

Are those tears? Stop or we'll drown.

Rudolph: Don't spoil it.

Sorry, I'm just so excited. I feel dizzy.

I don't know anymore...

Where am I? What am I doing?

Rudolph, I need to go.

Rudolph: Are you sure? Let's look at each other in that mirror. Aren't we beautiful together?

Yes. Yes, we are. I love you and want to stay with you.

C'mon, they're waiting for us.

Rudolph: You sure about that?

I am now. So many emotions in little time have tested even the strength of a weirdo like me. Please understand though that I'll need some time to calm down once the celebration's over, otherwise I doubt I'll survive this month.

Rudolph: It's a bit much for me too, and I predict more to come. But that changes nothing, as I want to feel every moment of this with you.

C'mon lazybones, we've got some vows to recite. Hurry!

Rudolph: You're fantastic.

...

Rudolph: Of course I do!

July 10 1926, 5:17 pm

I'm now Mrs. Valentino! Well, Guglielmi actually.

Where's the reception?

Rudolph: Tomorrow, at our new house.

"Our" house! That's so damn cool! Erm, I mean, it's nice to hear "our" used as an adjective.

Are we going to Frank's to celebrate?

Rudolph: Sure, just change clothes.

Of course! I'm so excited I forgot I'm still wearing the wedding dress.

What an unforgettable day July 10 1926 has turned out to be.

Why are you scowling?

Rudolph: You were staring at me.

So?

Rudolph: I don't know.

You're scowling again. Are you embarrassed or something? How can the great Rudolph Valentino be embarrassed about any-thing?

Rudolph: Alright, I am. Just don't include it in the book.

I want to be alone with you today. I don't want to see anyone else. I just want you to know that everything will be alright. I must protect you from everything. After all, you're not from this time. You'd be lost without me.

Wait here.

Turn that board around.

You are my world

I can't believe you wrote that.

You're crazy!

You're so sweet. Let's eat and go home.

Give me the board.

Rudolph: Show me what you've written.

I will Always Love You

July 10 1926, 10:30 pm

The stars are beautiful even in LA. How couldn't they be, on a day like this?

They look like pulsating gems.

I'm happy, so very happy.

I feel everything Rudolph does. It's as if I've lived a lifetime in just a few days, and it's only just beginning!

Too bad tomorrow I won't be able to say who I am at the party.

Who cares? At least *we* know.

It would be a shame if all of this was just a story in a book.

I'll go and find him in the garden.

July 11 1926, 7:00 pm

I'm ready. I bet he'll faint when he sees me.

I've never worn anything so sensual before. It really does justice to my figure.

I almost look like an actress.

I must hurry. The first guests are arriving.

The only problem is that Pola Negri is among them. I know it's absurd, but I'm jealous, considering she thinks she'll be the third Mrs. Valentino!

I must put on a brave face and make sure he looks only at me. I think attracting the attention of the other men should do the trick. I'm heading upstairs and I'm a ball of nerves. I feel like a schoolgirl before an exam. My head's spinning. I must focus. I can't faint just now.

Rudolph: Okay, keep calm. Don't mouth off suddenly. Remember, we're relatives now.

I know.

Rudolph: *Not in that sense. Don't confuse things. I have to introduce you now.*

What do you need to remember?

To keep my emotions in check, I know.

Rudolph: *Good. Let's go.*

Hey, isn't that Charlie Chaplin?

Rudolph: *What did you just promise me?*

Yes, sorry.

Rudolph: *It's a good thing you don't know what he's saying.*

What?

Rudolph: *He wanted to know if you were an actress, then asked me something which is typical of him.*

Which is?

Rudolph: *He asked if you were single.*

Wow! We should exchange cell numbers.

Rudolph: *Very funny.*

Come, let's see if you're still grinning when I present you to Pola Negri.

Why shouldn't I grin? You don't think I'm jealous, do you?

Rudolph: *I hope you aren't.*

Well you'll never know. We women should always maintain some air of mystery.

Rudolph: *That's a shame. I would have liked it if you were.*

If you think you can gauge my thoughts by provoking me, then you don't really know me.

Wow, there are beautiful women everywhere. Mary Pickford, Vilma Banky, Mea Murray... Thank God there's her partner Douglas Fairbanks and, last but not least, Buster Keaton.

I thought this party would be exciting, but I'm bored to death. I can't understand what anyone's saying, and Rudolph's not helping. At least I can talk to Chaplin.

Chaplin: Hey Rudolph, I spent the whole evening with your cousin who, among other things, speaks English. Not terribly well, but... Getting back on topic, I offered her some wine and peaches, but it turns out she can't handle them very well. She actually told me that you two are married, and that your name's Raffaello.

Rudolph: She's a teetotaler, and Raffaele's her fiancé. I'll take her to bed. Thank you for telling me.

Chaplin: My pleasure. I'd love to see her again in a touch less inebriated state. Would that be possible?

Rudolph: I'll ask her tomorrow.

Chaplin: I would be grateful if you did.

Rudolph: So, how are you?

Well. Why?

Rudolph: Have you drunk something?

Yes, Charlie offered me something, and I could hardly refuse. I tasted it, just to avoid causing offence. Then I saw you with Pola Negri, linking arms with her throughout the night. I felt so alone and so unwanted that one glass became two, then three. Why did you let her touch you?

Rudolph: Everyone suspects there's something going on between us. I had to do something to make them think otherwise.

You could have done so without getting me mixed up in this farce.

This should have been our celebration. Instead it was only mine, and I made a fool of myself.

Rudolph: I was just about to say that, but you're so good at pissing me off.

Go to Hell, Guglielmi! Drunk or not, I'm going to sleep in another room. I ask you to kindly not disturb me. Heck, why don't you sleep with Negri? If you're going to play a part, get in character.

He took my words literally. He's gone. I just hope he hasn't gone sleeping around. What will happen now? I can't go home and I feel so alone, but most of all hurt and unloved. One minute you're on top the world, the next...
I'm going to cry.
I'm still dressed, so I can go outside and think.
I hope there'll be no one there.
I'll leave tomorrow. I'll take the flapper-style clothes he gave me and go. Our bedroom is fortunately empty. I couldn't have stood seeing him in bed with another woman. I need to stay focused.
I'm here to get my clothes, that's all.
Shoes, purse, that should be all.
The suitcase is packed. I'm going now. My mood isn't any better, but I'd like to see the stars from his beautiful garden one last time.
My love for him is intense but, as is the nature of such things, it has changed as abruptly as it began.
I know crying won't solve anything, but it will help me vent.
I want to go back to 2015.
Rudolph: How can you even think about leaving? Where would you go?
I'm not staying where I'm not wanted and am replaced by someone else the day after my marriage, where feelings that could turn the world upside down vanish before the charms of another woman. I'm worth something, not somebody's play-thing. In any case, I must ask you to not get in my way. I'll be gone tomorrow anyway. Just help me find someone who'll employ me, so that I can survive in this time. I miss my family and I want to go home.
Rudolph: You're right. How could I expect you to understand the perversity of this world? A world of movie stars and divas where traditional values are ephemeral. How could I have given so much importance to it? I don't deserve you. I knew it wouldn't have lasted.

I'll have you taken tomorrow to an acquaintance of mine. He'll give you everything you need.

Asshole!

Rudolph: Where are you running to?

I'm getting out of here. Wake someone up who'll accompany me or I'll leave by foot. Go one, move!

Rudolph: What are you even talking about? You can't.

Screw you and your pessimism.

Get on with it!

A real asshole through and through. He's actually gone to call someone.

How could I have let myself get fooled by a movie star, a guy who can have however many women he wants. Why didn't he just leave me alone? I can't wait to leave. I feel like I've been stabbed in the heart.

I'm going to faint. No, please, not now.

July 12 1926, 10:00 am

Where am I?

I've never seen this room before. Where has he taken me?

I look out of the window and recognize Santa Monica. I must be back in the Falcon Lair. The bed is covered in lilies. Strange.

There are even some rose petals.

I wish everything would return to how it was before.

I miss everything about him. I don't want it to end like this. I want to hold him to me and find my happiness again.

Maybe these lilies are his way of showing me he hasn't stopped loving me.

I'll sneak up on him in our room and kiss him to death.

Good morning Mariella. Is Mister Valentino in our room?

Mariella: He's out at the moment, but he shouldn't be gone long.

Thank you.

I'll have a lie down and wait for him.

I'm going in.

What the...? You bastard!

I'm taking a shower and leaving.

This whole affair is making me sick. My stomach can't take it anymore. It's as if I'm pregnant.

Mariella, sorry, but is there another cab I can take?

Mariella: Certainly, I'll call one right away.

I mustn't cry. I must put on a brave face. I can't, it's all too much. That damn pig!

Goodbye Falcon Lair. I'll miss you.

Good morning Luca.

Take me to Musso & Frank's Grill please.

Luca: Right away, ma'am.

Please drive as quickly from here as possible.

Rudolph: Mariella, where's Anna?

Mariella: She's gone. She asked about you when she got up. I told her you'd be back soon, so she decided to wait for you in the bedroom. When she opened the door she went pale and ran off all hysterical. She asked to be taken to Musso & Frank's Grill, all teary eyed. Luca's taking her there.

Rudolph: Wait, why was she hysterical?

Mariella: We haven't refurbished the room yet sir.

Rudolph: Dammit! She misunderstood, that's why!

Mariella: May I advise you sir to not drive too fast when pursuing her? It wouldn't do anybody any good if you had an accident.

Rudolph: Thank you Mariella. You're the wisest person I know. Your counsel's always appreciated.

I didn't expect her to get up so early. I'm on my way, my love. Just don't do anything rash. You can't handle this. You don't know anything about this period, and you could come to harm. You've no idea how much I miss you.

The road between us seems to go on forever. Lord, please protect her. I wouldn't be able to live with myself if something happened. I can't live an hour without her.

How could I be so dumb, such an "asshole" as she said?

God, I beg you, watch over her. Let get to her in time to explain everything.

I implore you.

I've arrived. This parking lot will do fine.

Frank, where's Anna?

Frank: She went just a few minutes ago. She left her suitcase, saying she's be back to fetch it.

Rudolph: Did she tell you where she was going

Frank: No. She was crying, and I couldn't understand a word she was saying. I did however see her take the road on the right.

Rudolph: Thanks Frank. I'd better get moving.

Here she comes! But wait, there's a car coming too.

No! She's crossing the road and hasn't noticed it.

Rudolph: I feel like I've fallen from the sky. How are you feeling, Anna?

We're on the floor and my arm hurts. How do you think I feel? Why did you do that?

Rudolph: You were about to be flattened.

I guess it's my destiny to be constantly rescued.

I'm still pissed off, but I suppose I should thank you.

Rudolph: You can do that by listening to what I have to say.

Here, let me help you up.

Your eyes are red. Your silence isn't helping in breaking the tension.

That's not my Anna.

Listen to me.

I also had a drop too many last night. Not being a habitual drinker, I lost my faculties. Seeing you with Charlie clouded my mind. It was as if I didn't exist. When Pola started flirting, I thought nothing of it. Indeed, I thought it would do you good to see how crazy women are about me.

Then you started saying really hurtful stuff in the garden, and left.

After all I'd done for you!

At that point, I ran to my room and threw myself in bed.

I won't lie to you: I cried. I saw your pillow and snuggled up to it.

I missed you so much. I didn't want you to leave, so I decided that once I got up, I'd go and get a picnic basket and finally taken you to the beach.

When I woke up, Mariella told me that you'd gone into our room and run out crying. I retraced your steps, trying to work out what

*could have shocked you that badly. Then I realized that you
thought there was a woman sleeping on your side of the bed.*
How could such a thought come to you?
What do you take me for?
Some insensitive monster?
*Even the best actor in the world could never have played such a
part for that length of time.*
*Why can't you just stop and think once in a while instead of act-
ing on impulse?*
I love you. Do you really think I'd be capable of such a thing?
What would you have thought in my shoes?
Wouldn't you have come to the same conclusion?
*Rudolph: I don't know, but I like to think I'd have been more
trusting and asked for an explanation.*
Funny, I remember you wanting me to leave.
*Rudolph: I never did or said I did. You were the one who wanted
to go.*
Women never truly think what they say when angry. The whole
drama's about giving the man the opportunity to resolve every-
thing. From what I've seen, you were too ignorant to know that!
Rudolph: I was too drunk.
From now on, no more wine.
Rudolph: Obviously.
Can you forgive me?
Your excuse makes sense, but I've suffered too much.
These explanations are a little late, and I find it hard to trust
you.
*Rudolph: Close your eyes and give me your hand. Put it on my
heart. What do you feel?*
Your hearts racing and you're breathing's shallow. You're scared,
aren't you?
Rudolph: Yes, you've no idea how much I am.
If I'm guilty of something, it's being an idiot.
Please, recall everything we've done together.
Remember when we went to Frank's?
The new house?
The first time we made love in Falcon Lair?

Yes, in the bathtub.
I think I get it now.
Even with a worried face, you're adorable.
Now what?
Rudolph: Let's go back to Frank's, fill up the basket I've just bought and head to the beach. Oh, let's not forget your suitcase too.
But I don't have my swimsuit!
Rudolph: So?

July 12 1926, 1:00 pm

The sea!
I'm still a little shaken, but now at least I know the dangers our love faces.
Resting my head on his shoulder makes everything seem normal again. By normal, I don't mean "normality" in the strictest sense, but a calmness which rocks you to sleep.
Why are you stopping?
Rudolph: I don't feel well.
Is it the ulcer?
Rudolph: Yes. The pain's really bad.
Shouldn't we get you operated?
Rudolph: Not yet.
Rudolph, look at me!
Do you trust me?
I'll drive.
Rudolph: No, not the Voisin!
Ah, you've recovered already!
You take your cars seriously.
Rudolph: I do. I've bought a really awesome one which is now hidden in the garage. I wanted it to be a surprise.
A third Isotta?
Rudolph: Close enough.
This isn't your usual way of expressing yourself.
Rudolph: Please, forget everything!

Are you changing subject on me? Are you talking about our fight?
Rudolph: Yes.
Maybe. I'll think about it.
Rudolph: Hold it! I know, you're about to do that eyebrow thing.
And you've suddenly got better.
Rudolph: You're amazing.
Let's stop here. It's peaceful, and I imagine Santa Monica's quite crowded at this hour.
Rudolph: And why not!
You should have continued with the compliments.
Rudolph: I thought you'd get bored of them.
Why are you laughing?
For a Latin Lover, you certainly don't understand women all that well! We constantly misunderstand each other, despite talking the same language.
Are you stripping down? You're butt-naked!
Rudolph: You ought to be used to it by now. Remember the lake?
They'll have seen your dongle even now.
Rudolph: And what was it like?
Typical.
Rudolph: Of a Latin Lover?
I'm not sure about that, but it was certainly unique.
Rudolph: I should hope so. Well?
Well, when we get home I'll grab a ruler and measure you.
Rudolph: You deserve a smack on the ass.
Dive in. I want to teach you to swim.
I swim perfectly well.
Rudolph: You should have answered yes, then pretended to drown so I could come and rescue you.
That way, you'd make me feel heroic.
Don't be silly. I know all the swimming styles and could probably beat you anyway.
Rudolph: Whatever. I give up.
I'm drowning! Oh Rudolph, help me!
Rudolph: Very convincing...

But I've caught my foot between two rocks! Please, come quick-
ly!
Rudolph: It's true! Hold on, I'm coming.
Thanks Rudolph. You're my hero of the day.
*Rudolph: There you go with your eyebrow again! You little liar,
you're not going to get away with this!*
Remember what I did to the thief.
Rudolph: Screw it, that's the last thing on my mind.
You shouldn't use that language in the twenties.
Rudolph: I'll show you what a twenties guy can do!
Hey, wheezy!
Aren't I supposed to be the asthmatic one?
*Rudolph: Sure, but I'm out of shape today. Tomorrow I'll be un-
beatable.*
If you say so.

July 15 1926, 9:00 pm

These days have been amazing. It's like we're kids again. Except
for some fainting, I don't think I've ever been so energetic in all
my life.
He's so sweet. I can relax and have fun with him. It's just like be-
ing in a romantic novel.
Let's hope we can publish these writings. I sometimes wonder if
this gadget around my neck really is a microphone, and how it
can record so many hours.
I'll demand an explanation when August 23 comes and goes!
I need to trust him. Now I'll leave a little message to my family.
Let's see...
Hi mom, hi dad. I think this is the only way I can reach you.
I've changed my name in this book in order to be more easily
recognized.
Dad, you've always known how much the twenties interest me.
You gave me all those projectors and other things from that pe-
riod, but I imagine you never dreamed I could travel through
time.
Even I find it somewhat absurd.

156

By the time you read this, I'll have been dead for years, so read carefully what I'm about to say.

I am so very happy. I was happy even with Claudio, who I remember with joy. We'd become distant in the last few years, but I always held some affection for him. I'll be honest, I miss him and wish he'd find someone who loves him, just as I did for years.

This doesn't change how I feel about Rudolph though. I am deeply in love with him. I can't deny it, and I think you'll agree, having read this book so far.

I hope you're having fun with your friends.

Mom, you must know that I don't take medication anymore, though I can't explain why.

I've never felt better.

I hope my relationship with Rudolph lasts. You can be sure of one thing: my life with Rudolph will be full of love, serenity and no money problems. Knowing what is to come in 1929 will help me organize financially.

I love you. Never forget that.

A big hug from the past.

Anna.

I'm off to bed now. Tomorrow we'll organize our next trip.

I'll finally get to know New York.

I'll cry when I leave Falcon Lair. I know it's just a house, but it's become part of my new life, and I'll miss it.

Goodnight.

July 16 1926, 4:00 pm

We're about to take the train to New York.

I feel energized at the sole thought of seeing that city.

Seeing it in this time period simply adds more spice to this story. Too bad they've yet to build the Empire State Building. Never mind. We'll come back in 1931 when it's done. The journey is very long, and Rudolph has booked a cabin with bunks. It will take six days to get there, as we're going to stop for a few days in Chicago.

It will be my name-day soon, and he's given me a jewel-encrusted Cartier fountain pen.

Rudolph has impeccable taste. He'll have to restrain himself when we get back though. He's something of a spendthrift!

July 22 1926, 8:00 pm

I'm in New York! It saddens me that I can't tell my friends about it.

I miss you all! That's how I feel about you, and I hope I've managed to convey the sincerity of my words through this book.

Rudolph: Aren't I enough for you?

Sorry, that's not what I meant. Wouldn't you feel a little lonely in my place?

Rudolph: Yes, but I'd forget about it just by looking at you.

You always know how to cheer me up!

Rudolph: Now let's go to the Ambassador Hotel. We need to rest. I'll take you to Tiffany's tomorrow.

Why there?

Rudolph: I saw the clock you keep on your desk and realized it was from Tiffany's. I thought you'd like to visit it.

I'd prefer to see the Statue of Liberty. I've seen it in photos, and would love to admire it in person.

I want to feel what you did when you saw it for the first time.

Will we come back and see it after August 23?

Rudolph: Yes, my love.

Once we get to our room, I'll need to introduce you to my assistant. Remember, I told him not to come to LA because I wanted to spend as much time with you as possible. Now he'll be of great help in this period.

I remember. Yes, okay.

If I look a little distracted, it's because I'm nervous.

Rudolph: Relax. Everything will be all right.

You know it's more complicated than that.

Rudolph: Yes ma'am, but I want to always see you smile. I know the pain I feel sometimes manifests on my face. That boxing match I took part in shortly before I met you only made it worse.

158

But we're here now, ready to start our new future.
Here comes my assistant.
This is Anna.
Nice to meet you.
Rudolph: He'll take you back to LA after August 23.
Alright.
Rudolph: Go to sleep now. I have a lot to talk about with him.
Give me a goodnight kiss.
See you tomorrow.
The days pass too quickly and my excitement is giving way to fear. I must put on a brave face and not transmit my anxiety to him.

These could very well be his last days on Earth, I don't want him to spend them worrying about me.
Goodnight.

July 23 1926, 10:00 am

We're trying to get to the Statue of Liberty, but there are road-works going on, so it's impossible to reach. Roadblocks are everywhere, and I can barely catch a glimpse of it.
Never mind, Rudolph. We can visit it another time.
Rudolph: C'mon you lazy baby boomer, I need to show you something big.
I don't want to.
Oh, now I get it. We're running because there's someone following us.
Rudolph: It won't happen again after the 23rd.
I hope so. We're not twenty anymore.
Rudolph: Come in here.
Sorry, but can I hug you?
Strange, you've never needed my permission before.
Rudolph: Be quiet.
Woah, that was one hell of a kiss.
Rudolph: Why are you puckering your lips like that?
Kiss me again.
Wow, my lips are tingling. It was as if you wanted to eat them.

Rudolph: I was only fooling around. Now let's get serious.
Too bad we can only kiss behind this door.
Rudolph: Let's go upstairs. A friend of mine lives here.
Then what?
Rudolph: Don't worry, it's not what you think it is. It's just that I haven't seen him in a while and want to say hi.
Please don't include his name in the book.
Alright.
Rudolph: Let's knock.
Is Mister _ home?
Doorman: Yes Mister Valentino. Make yourself comfortable. I'll tell him you've arrived.
Rudolph: Thank you.
What a lovely house. Is he an important man?
Rudolph: Yes, very.
The house built in the Liberty style. The chandeliers are very elegant, and the brightness of the colors harkens back to the last century.
There's a huge bear rug next to the fireplace. Close by is a small armchair behind a Chinese style coffee table, which is very fashionable these days. It must be very relaxing to read in this room, warmed by the burning firewood.
I can smell something coming from the kitchen.
I'm hungry.
Rudolph, my stomach's growling.
Rudolph: We can't exactly come in unannounced only to demand lunch.
I'd know how to.
Rudolph: That I don't doubt. Get a grip.
Host: Hello Rudolph. I didn't know you had company. Are you going to present her to me or what?
Rudolph: This is Anna.
Pleased to meet you.
Host: I guess Rudolph hid you in order to avoid attracting rivals.
That's very kind of you, but you're mistaken. Rudolph and I are just friends.
Host: Please, sit. I hope you'll join me for lunch.

I'm not sure. We have other plans.

Rudolph: They can wait. It would be an honor to accept. It will give us the chance to catch up.

Host: I shall get everything set then.

I'm surprised at just how many Italians there are here. How was I?

Rudolph: Just perfect! I feared you'd be too direct, but you managed to let me do all the decision-making.

In my days, we'd probably be considered freeloaders. We turned up unannounced for lunch after all.

Rudolph: We're friends, so it doesn't matter. In any case, we'd be considered freeloaders here too.

Host: When did you arrive?

Rudolph: We've been here since yesterday.

Host: We?

Rudolph: Yes. Anna lives in Los Angeles too. She needed to come to New York on business, so we traveled together. I offered to show her around today.

Host: I see. You haven't smoked anything since coming here. Have you stopped or something?

Rudolph: I have. Most people can't stand the smell.

Host: Do you smoke, Anna?

No, I hate it.

Host: I understand.

Rudolph: Bought some new canvas?

Host: No. No time, and politics is a real chore. Please, let's get started.

You're awfully quiet, Anna.

I'm just admiring your house. I find every detail fascinating.

Host: You can thank my wife for making it the way it is. Unfortunately time seems to have stopped since her passing. People you love may die, but their memory doesn't. Hers will forever be stamped on everything surrounding us now. Time won't wash away the beautiful moments we spent together.

She was special, and her absence doesn't change that. You'd understand if you were in love.

I am, in a way I've never been before.

But I find it hard to believe you could recover from such a loss.
Host: I never did. My life simply gave me the resources to cope. I'm a survivor.
Let's not dwell on this further. Tell me something about the world of celluloid.
So, Rudolph, I hear your new movie's coming out.
Rudolph: Yes, in September. It's called The Son of the Sheik.
Host: I heard your movies will soon have sound.
Rudolph: Indeed. I'm going to a rehearsal soon. My admirers will be able to hear my voice in the next instalment.
Host: Do you know what the plot will be?
Rudolph: I can't say.
Host: Classified?
Rudolph: Need to know basis....

August 15 1926, 7:00 pm

I've finally managed to get some water bottles for Rudolph. Oh shoot, I've dropped them. I got a chill and they just fell out of my arms. Weird.

Time flies in New York. It's a little chaotic, but exceptionally lively. Even the architecture's captivating. It merits a visit no matter what time period you're in.

Assistant: Come quickly. I've called an ambulance. Mister Valentino just collapsed. He's alive, but it looks serious.

Ask the doctors where they'll take him and I'll take a cab.

Rudolph, can you hear me? Answer me, my love. It's me.

Don't fool around with me, look at me.

Wake up!

Speak to me!

My God, this is really happening.

No! This can't be true. This can't happen.

Get up, we need to go back to LA.

Come on, we need to make love.

Please, just react.

You can't do this to me. Don't think even for one minute that you can just leave me here in 1926. I beg you, wake up.

My love.
Assistant: They've arrived.
No, I don't want to.
Assistant: Come, let's take a cab to the Polyclinic Hospital.
Wait, let me get my purse. I need vitamins!

August 16 1926, 5:00 am

Assistant: They said they need to operate. It's his ulcer.
Thanks. Keep me informed please.
This waiting is too much for me. I know the surgery will go well, but I'm still worried. I just hope I can get to him and give him his vitamins.
God, please help us.
I don't know how long I've been waiting here. I think it must be Monday at eight in the evening.
I've finally been told that the surgery was a success, but I'm not allowed to see him. Everything's so confused. Doctors and nurses rush in and out of his room. My mind's a blur, but I must find a way to get to him.

Tuesday August 17 1926, 12:00 pm

I haven't eaten for days, but I must drink something.
Nurse: Anna Piccolini!
That's me. I'll raise my hand in case she doesn't understand. No, I feel faint. I'll put the antibiotics in my bra…
Where am I? They're looking over me. They're smiling and hugging me. I don't understand what they're saying, but they seem happy. I just hope they'll take me to Rudolph.
What's the nurse telling Rudolph?
Rudolph: Hello my love.
Don't speak.
How do I look? Bad?
Don't give me that look. Remember you need to give me the antibiotics.
Here they are.

163

Rudolph: You need to get well, or that wax model made to impersonate me during the vigil won't be worth a damn.
I'll take the next pill in twenty hours just to be safe. I need to get my strength back.
The nurse told me something big.
What?
Rudolph: I now have an additional reason to live. I'm going to be a father?
Who's the lucky lady?
Now's not the time to argue.
Rudolph: It's you, silly.
That's impossible, and you know it.
Rudolph: How old do you look?
I don't know, but younger than I actually am.
Rudolph: I'll explain later. You are indeed younger, and are now expecting our child. You're going to be a mommy!
What am I going to do? Will you be there with me?
Rudolph: Don't worry. Everything will be okay.
Kiss me. You must go now. My assistant will take you to Los Angeles, then you'll take the train home.
I don't want to go. I want to stay with you. Please...
Rudolph: You can't, but you can be sure of one thing: I will return to you.
Nothing can prevent me.
Now I must rest.
Go, my love. Please, be strong for both of us, or rather, all three of us.
I will love you till I breathe my last. I'll wait for you. You're the love of my life.
Rudolph: You've made me the happiest man on Earth.
Kiss me and go.

August 23 1926, 12:15 pm

Please Lord, I need to know if he's alive.
All the biographies I've read say that he should be dead by now.
I must know the truth. He can't just disappear from my life.

What will become of our child?

I'm not ready for this.

What will I do if it gets sick?

Maybe Rudolph worries about the same things. At least we'd face them together.

God, please, let him live!

I beg you, don't take him away from me.

I know I shouldn't fret, but I feel like I'm losing my mind.

I miss you so much.

I miss your caresses, your way of holding me and joking. The worst part will be not being able to laugh with you, and have our child hear us.

I need to calm down. You'll see, little one. Mom will know what to do, and you'll grow up healthy, strong, and just as beautiful as your father.

Guglielmi, wherever you are, you'll be proud of me.

I'll love you forever.

September 23 1926, 3:00 pm

Look at all these bills! Studying bookkeeping has certainly come in useful. Agriculture was a problem to get to grips with, but I'm almost an expert now. I can even name the lunar cycles. A full moon appeared two days ago, and now we're at the last quarter which began on the 28th of this month. I'm proud of my work and the basic knowledge I've gained in building our child's new world. Cultivating the earth is exhausting work, but at least there's Giovanni.

I've neglected continuing the book, but now it's time to conclude it. I'm getting used to this pregnancy, and I've even stopped fainting. I want my baby to feel the same joy we did.

The only mystery is this microphone.

There, I'll press on of these buttons and see what happens.

Oh my God! It's Rudolph.

It's as if he's really here. I don't understand. I can see him, but he's not a movie projection. He's standing right before me, but I can't touch him. Could it be a hologram? In 1926?

What is this "thing"?

It's talking…

Hello my love. I'm watching you as you walk through the fields. You're as curious as always. I don't know if I'll be coming back from New York, so…

I can't take it. God help me, I miss him so badly. I can't carry on. He recorded this when he took me here for the first time, on July 4th I think.

Give me the strength, Lord.

My love, if our child's a boy, I'll call him Rudolph. It can't be any other way.

Rudolph: No, we'll call him Alberto, like my brother.

Rudolph, it's you. You've come back.

Rudolph: Stop it, you'll knock me over.

But are you…

Dead?

Or alive?

Rudolph: Alive.

To be continued…..

PS: I thank my husband Roberto Puma for his support in the realization of this book.

Maria Pasquinelli for having been my proof-reader.

Rodolfo Guglielmi for having inspired this purely fantastical book.

> *Rodolfo: Do you think the women reading this book will find me arousing?*
>
> *Anna: Who knows...!*

Sitography

http://www.rudolph-valentino.com/ Site on the life of Rudolph Valentino and the Falcon Lair house curated by Donna Hill 1997-2011. URL accessed 3 May 2015.
https://en.wikipedia.org/wiki/Rudolph_Valentino Article on Rudolph Valentino. URL accessed 1 May 2017.
http://www.beltranmasses.com/biografia-beltran-masses/ Site which covers the life and works of Federico Beltran Masses. URL accessed 30 June 2015.
https://en.wikipedia.org/wiki/Louis_Sullivan Article on Louis Sullivan's architecture. URL accessed 1 May 2017.
 http://www.treccani.it/enciclopedia/frank-lloyd-wright/ Article on Frank Lloyd's architecture. URL accessed 5 July 2015.
https://en.wikipedia.org/wiki/Robie_House Article on Robie House in Chicago. URL accessed 1 May 2017.
http://www.scuoladeisapori.it/ Information regarding Chef Roberto Puma's cookery courses. URL accessed 4 May 2014.
http://mussoandfrank.com/history/ History of Musso & Frank Grill. URL accessed 1 July 2015.
http://www.movies.com/actors/rudolph-valentino/rudolph-valentino-movies/p284767 Several of Rudolph Valentino's movies. URL accessed 6 May 2014.
http://www.tcm.com/tcmdb/title/326475/The-Son-of-the-Sheik/ Notes on "The son of the Sheik". URL accessed 10 July 2015.

Glossary of 2015 terminology

Cellphone: Small wireless telephone.

Computer: Descendant of the typewriter and the difference engine, featuring a kaleidoscope-like screen upon which one can see what one writes and searches for on the internet.

Dishwasher: Device which permits the washing of cutlery and ceramics without human intervention. Invented in 1924 by William Howard Livens, it operates on electricity and has yet to see widespread use.

Dyane: French car model.

E-mail: Post sent via internet.

Facebook: Personal public diary shared via internet.

File: Written document which can be re-read, modified or printed whenever necessary.

Google: Large library which can be consulted on a computer.

Highway: A road with numerous bifurcations requiring toll payments for access.

Hodgepodge: A mix of ingredients haphazardly mixed together.

Hologram: Image of a person or object projected into empty space without the necessity of a screen. Similar to a real person or object, but lacking physicality.

Intercom: Device installed outside buildings permitting communication with the people within.

Internet: Descendant of the telegraph with a central archive containing information accessible by computer.

Local health center: Supervisory body which makes sure hygienic standards are respected during food production.

Microphone: Descendant of the wax strip recorder.

MP3 (player): Small gramophone capable of playing a variety of different recorded musical arrangements.

Program: Method by which a computer is used.

Service station: Building situated on highways where one can refuel motor vehicles.

Skype: Telephone present on the computer permitting not only communication but also the possibility of seeing the speaker on a screen.

Tab: Computer page.
Tablet: Computer of small size.
Technician: A user of computers.
WhatsApp: Textual communication system present on cell phones.
Word: Computer program permitting all aforementioned activities.
YouTube: Film archive which can be accessed on the internet.

Finito di stampare nel mese di Luglio 2017
per conto di Youcanprint *Self-Publishing*